# Mumbo

# Jumbo

## Kathryn Lasky Knight

SUMMIT BOOKS

NEW YORK • LONDON • TORONTO

SYDNEY • TOKYO • SINGAPORE

**SUMMIT BOOKS**
SIMON & SCHUSTER BUILDING
ROCKEFELLER CENTER
1230 AVENUE OF THE AMERICAS
NEW YORK, NEW YORK 10020

10 9 8 7 6 5 4 3 2 1

LIBRARY OF CONGRESS CATALOGING IN PUBLICATION DATA
KNIGHT, KATHRYN LASKY.
MUMBO JUMBO / KATHRYN LASKY KNIGHT.
P.   CM.
I. TITLE.
PS3561.N485M86   1991
813'.54—DC20
                                                    91-2546
                                                    CIP
ISBN 0-671-68448-5

POEM ON PP. 108 AND 124 COMES FROM *ALLIGATOR PIE* BY DENNIS LEE
(BOSTON, MASSACHUSETTS: HOUGHTON MIFFLIN, 1974, P. 13).

*A great deal of intelligence is invested in ignorance when the need for illusion is great.*

—SAUL BELLOW

**1**————————— The figure had just emerged from the eroded streambed leading a burro. It paused for a moment by a saguaro cactus, fumbled in one pocket, then another. There were two small sounds: the click of a lighter and the soft rustle of paper, old paper, being unfolded. In the glow of the lighter the old man's face cut a profile as jagged as the outcrop behind him. He jammed the paper, a map, under his arm and fumbled in his pocket again, this time drawing out a pair of reading spectacles. He put them on and shoved back his hat. It was narrow-brimmed and had a low crown, Charlie Russell style, with a bunch of feathers sticking out of the band. He studied the map, made a soft grunt at it, clicked the lighter shut, and folded up the map.

"C'mon," he growled, and proceeded up the gradual incline of the streambed. He mumbled . . . single words mostly, or sometimes a few strung together, raggedy scraps floating out into the predawn Arizona sky. The fragments could have been part of a dialogue, for there were pauses, and answers and pieces of questions and exclamations—"Archie, gonna be piss-ass 'bout this . . . not as piss-ass as you are 'bout Claudie . . . Claudie, I keep tell' you not to take off like that . . . Doc says . . . what do they know . . . friggin' Docs? . . . Goddam medicine give me raises hell with my gut . . . some choice—fartin' or forgettin' . . . 'course she got a lot of corners to this land—more than four—that's the way it came back then . . . Desert Land Act . . . nothin' done 'bout it till Harry S. . . . Roosevelt . . . not Archie . . . oh boy, piss-ass he be. . . ."

A quarter of an hour later the figure appeared high on a ridge dark against the early lavender of the sky. A low dark whisper of wind came up, scraping around the red rocks, coaxing them into spires, turrets, crests, and arches. In another ten minutes the sun like a bloodstained egg yolk would spill over the rim of the earth, but Tonk Cullen wouldn't see it. His hearing wasn't too good anymore. His sniffer was, though, and the smell cut right through the spice of the juniper and the sagebrush—a low-down sweet smell. Ain't no natural smell, he thought. Who the hell is so piss-ass stupid they'd track upwind? Then something snapped across his leg . . . and he felt it all happening so slowly and so unstoppably. Let go the burro, he commanded himself. Before he pitched over the rim he thought of the sun about to rise . . . first one he'd miss. . . .

**2** —————— It was hot. It was clammy and hot the way only Boston could get. The weathermen talked about "convections," "Bermuda highs," "elusive lows," "trapped air," "stalemated maritime systems." What it all boiled down to, almost literally boiled down to, was that a hot wind had been driven up to New England and then a bunch of crap from the Southeast had slammed into that. So the air was thick with fog and tidal smells, and it all sat on Boston for days, endless days. Flights were diverted to Providence or Hartford, air conditioners throbbed constantly, people drove with their car lights on in the daytime in June. And even in this supposedly coolest corner of Cambridge, once called Norton Woods, where there were still immense trees—trees so old they had seen the likes of the James brothers, both Henry and William, and Emerson and Agassiz treading old brick sidewalks, and even an Adams or two—it was hotter than hinges. Calista Jacobs had never put air-conditioning in her Victorian shingle house because she liked to hear the sounds of birds, and besides, the Jacobses' house was cool by nature with its high plaster ceilings and triumvirate of venerable trees—a giant oak and two tupelos. But on this morning it was even too hot for the birds. So she was listening to the fog! The fog and a window fan that she had broken down and bought three days before. Robert J. Lurtsema, host of "Morning Pro Musica," was sighing, as he usually did, over the news, but he had promised something cool and refreshing in the form of Debussy piano preludes to be followed by Handel's *Water Music* in the next portion of the classical music program.

In the meantime the fan was sucking in the miasma of thick, humid air that hung outside the study window and Calista was at her drawing board inking in an English sheepdog, of all things! It wasn't fair that she was here in Cambridge drawing English sheepdogs for the ninetieth-year celebration of the publication of *Peter Pan* and that her son, Charley, and Archie, her man, were out in Arizona having fun! Apparently 101 degrees in zero humidity was invigorating, according to Charley, as opposed to 97 degrees in Cambridge with 90 percent humidity. The telephone rang. She picked it up.

It was her editor. "Oh, Janet!"

"How goes it?"

"*Peter Pan*, I presume?"

"You presume right."

"Well, it goes hot and humid. Why didn't you wait for the centennial celebration to come out with a new edition?"

"I told you, it's the centennial of the hospital to which Barrie willed all his royalties from the book."

"Not mine, I hope." The remark drew a chuckle from Janet. "Don't go thinking I'm a Scrooge," Calista continued. "I'm going to give part of mine to the nuclear-freeze movement with hopes that we can prevent World War III so that children can get normal childhood illnesses that hospitals can treat."

"You sound a tad grim this morning."

"It's hot, and I miss Charley and Archie."

"You'll be there soon."

"A week if I get these roughs done and off to you."

"Good girl."

"Listen, does Nana really have to be an English sheepdog?"

"What were your thinking of instead—a poodle?"

"No, something with less fur—maybe a Dalmatian. It's just too goddam hot to draw all this fur."

"But she's always been a sheepdog."

"Not necessarily. In the 1911 Scribner's edition, Bedford made her look more like a black Lab."

"Well, that's hairy."

"Sleeker. Not so hot-looking," Calista said.

"What does your Nana look like so far?"

"Bernadette Peters having a hot flash."

"Oooh! Calista, I love Bernadette Peters. She's so sexy and maternal and nurturing. I think she'll make a perfect Nana. Really, I can just imagine a canine translation of her looks. I adored her in *Sunday in the Park*. Oh, I bet this is going to be some book."

They chatted a bit more and then signed off. Calista got up, walked barefoot to her kitchen, and got herself another glass of iced tea. Back at her desk, she took a cookie from a tin box painted to look like the Victoria and Albert Museum.

*Peter Pan* was not a hard book to do, nothing like a fully illustrated picture book. For this edition she was only required to do eight full-color illustrations and fifteen pen-and-ink ones. She had all the faces worked out. Darling and Hook were, of course, alter egos of each other. The wimp turned monster; impotence being the flip side of tyranny. Therefore, Calista sketched the wimp, or Mr. Darling, to appear slightly foppish, with a waxed mustache and pomaded hair combed back from a sharp peak. For Hook, it all turned sinister. He wore a long beard; the mustache was a thick, scraggly affair above a perpetually snarled yet sensuous mouth. The pirate's hat was cocked for business, diguising any hairline whatsoever. One was impotent and a fool; the other had a hook, and it wasn't just a hand that he was missing—or so Calista thought. In any case, he was a very angry fellow.

There was only one face that could incorporate that kind of duality—Werner von Sackler, the man who had seduced her once upon a time, a year after she had been widowed, and then had nearly killed her son. He wouldn't sue. He was in prison, and besides, he could never prove it. She had clever ways of concealing verifiable identities in her work. She was such a consummate illustrator that she could capture the ineffable spirit, the soul, of a personality without ever mocking the physiognomy or drawing too close a likeness, setting up a line-for-line analogy. Archie, her lover for a year now, compared her to those geologists he worked with who could see through rock, as he said, and comprehend the fault lines, the silicate structure, almost intuitively.

Archie was in the book too. In her last book, *Marian's Tale*, she had used Archie's eyes, just his eyes, for Robin Hood. This time he would be Tiger Lily, the Indian princess captured by Hook's crew. When she reread the story in preparation and came to the part where Smee and Starkey were abducting her in the rowboat, she saw Barrie had written, "She was to be left on the rock to perish, an end to one of her race more terrible than death by fire or torture . . . yet her face was impassive; she was the daughter of a chief, she must die as a chief's daughter. . . ." It was the grace and stoicism that spelled "Archie" to Calista. She knew Tiger Lily's face had to be his, or rather a feminization of his wonderful face.

She looked at the picture she had on her drawing table, a photograph taken on his last birthday. He was the only man she knew who didn't look silly with a paper party hat on. His bold blue eyes, one winking at Calista, the other boring right into her from the picture frame—the face with its beautiful angularity, full of merriment. Oh Jeez! She missed him. The other picture on her desk was of Charley, her almost fourteen-year-old son. How relaxed his face had become in the last year, since Archie had entered their lives on a more or less permanent basis.

Despite his chores at the Smithsonian in Washington, Archie usually managed to spend every other weekend in Cambridge and often several weekdays if he were consulting with the Peabody Museum at Harvard. And starting next fall it would be more, as he would be a visiting professor in North American Archaeology.

That was where Charley and he were now—in Arizona digging paleo-Indian sites.

Charley, a computer prodigy, was writing a program for analysis of pottery sherds from what was known in the business of southwestern archaeology as the Mogollon-Anasazi period. Charley was serving them both well at the moment—computerizing Archie's sites and providing a face for Peter Pan. The face, or aspects of Charley's face, had threaded its way through much of Calista's work. Again it was not always recognizable as an exact likeness of Charley, but there was often an undeniable similarity. In the case of Peter Pan it was Charley as he had been a few years before, when he was closer to ten or eleven and still had vestiges of the little-boy contours to his face. His face within the last year and a half had become leaner, his jaw had squared off, his cheekbones had emerged, and there were no more apple cheeks.

Apparently, Calista thought to herself, she had something in common with Mrs. Darling—desperately trying to cling to her child! Was that not the source of the story's energy—this torsion between separation and growing up? Of course, Peter wanted it both ways, which was what made him such an enigmatic character—he ran away so he would never have to grow up. He became the boy who would never grow up but exist in some peculiar limbo and never be exactly a child or an adult, but totally sexless. Mr. Darling, although alter ego to Hook, was also in a sense the converse of Peter, for as in some bad joke, he had stayed home and never grown up. He remained strangely sexless. What a fascinating story. That was why Calista had leapt at the chance to illustrate it.

Growing up, separation between parents and children, was the great theme of children's literature—the child's need for independence versus the parent's need to cling. Calista took out a sketch of Peter she had done. It did look just as Charley had three years before. She'd better watch this, she thought, as a lot of complicated feelings scurried through her heart and brain.

Three more years and he'd be off to college! It was good that he was off now with Archie. She had become much too clinging in the almost four years since her husband's death. Archie had helped immensely.

It felt okay to let go a little bit now that she and Archie were together. She had learned better how to be alone. She didn't need to grab at her only child. In her worst moments, when the loneliness used to rack her with gale-force intensity, it was easy to imagine herself turning into a craven, pathetic character, indeed a James Barrie, who in his desperation had taken over an entire real-life family and manipulated them on the canvas of his work. For it was the Llewelyn-Davies family Barrie first met in Kensington Gardens that became the source of *Peter Pan*, his greatest work. The relationship between the artist and the boys developed into a mysterious and uneasy one. He became a manipulator of their personalities both on and off the pages of the book. It was creepy. Calista knew exactly what he had done. He had crossed over, failed to discriminate the differences between fantasy and reality.

But that wasn't Calista. As one of America's foremost illustrators of children's books, nobody understood the differences between fantasy and reality better than she did. She possessed a profound grasp of the finer discriminations between the two. So what the hell was she doing mooning over Charley's chubby little ten-year-old mug! She really didn't want him not to grow up or to remain ten years old forever—acneless, tractable, and adorable. No! Bring on those pimples, bring on those raging hormones, those pubescent funks!

She took out one of the rough sketches she had been working on. It showed Peter standing on a rock looking out across a stretch of sea. He had been left there wounded by Hook with a rising tide. Unable to fly or swim because of his wound, he was doomed. No artist since the 1911 edition had elected to illustrate this scene in the book. But Calista had. Her Peter stood cocky, his chest thrust out, his chin with a brave tilt just as Barrie had described—

"standing erect on the rock again, with that smile on his face and a drum beating within him. It was saying, 'To die will be an awfully big adventure.' "

# 3

Dear Mom,

Hope you get this letter in time. We tried to call you but you were out and as you know the nearest phone is 100 miles from where we are camped. I think you need to get one of those answer machines; Archie agrees. He says that you are the last person on earth not to have one. I think he's right. Anyhow, here's my shopping list . . . five bucks' worth of thermal coils #.3 size. You can get them at Tech City on Third Street in Cambridge. Also, I need .4 size but I have a few of these in the bottom drawer of my desk. There also might be some in a bag in my sock drawer. [I should ask why? thought Calista. Of course not. File under sock.] When you're at Tech City pick me up a dozen .7 volt power diodes and some 74569. integrated circuits. See if the Hall Effect Sensor has come in that I ordered aeons ago. If not, get them to lend you one of theirs; they said they would. Try to get Dave to help you. He's the one who stutters, but he's the only one who knows where anything is down there. Also in my room in a paper bag near Rambo's cage is a bunch of transistors. And there is a McDonald's Happy Meal box that has some resistors in it. Bring those, please. Bring my Deep Think floppy disks—they are all labeled. And last but not least bring the Time Slicer and Ozo printer. I think it's in the basement workshop. Why, I hear you saying it now, do we need the Time Slicer? You'll never guess. I'll give you a multiple-choice test. We need the Time Slicer because:

(1) Peter Gardiner has risen from the dead and is faking data again [Calista found this less than humorous].

(2) U.S. has yet again set off an unannounced underground

atomic explosion and I'm selling the story to *The National In-quirer.*

(3) A religious group thinks that God is speaking to them through little holes in the earth.

The answer is: number three. There is this incredibly weird group out here. They are centered at a ranch outside of Red Forks. It's called Rancho Radiance. They worship rainbows, believe that God's vibrations come out of these desert potholes that they call vortices. They claim it all has to do with mag-netic fields. But they don't call it magnetic. They call it the Yin field and it is supposed to be aligned to the female force and then they separate that from the electric field which they call the Yang field, for the male force. Yin Yang Ding Dong! Or, as Oscar the Grouch on "Sesame Street" says, "Ding Dong you're wrong." Their spiritual leader is this lady called Pahata Ra. Sounds Indian doesn't it? But Archie says she's no more Indian than he is. In any case Pahata Ra has made big bucks. She's got all these followers who I guess give her money and she flies around in a lavender jet—that's their favorite color. She also has two helicopters, but get this, this is the weirdest of all: She believes that she is the reincarnation of a 65,000-year-old woman from the steppes of Russia!

See you soon,
Love, Charley.

P.S. Say hi to Rambo for me. I won't ask you to kiss him.

"Hi, Rambo!" Calista called up to Charley's room. Rambo was Charley's hamster, and before she left to join Charley and Archie in Arizona she must remember to deliver him to Matthew, Charley's best friend. Calista folded the letter and put it in her pocket. Now what the heck was Charley going to do with the Time Slicer once he got it out there with these vortices? And what kind of moisturizer did a 65,000-year-old woman use? Lan-côme Niosome cream? That's what Calista used just the other side of forty. She supposed that after the first millennium one had to beef it up a bit in terms of moisturizers. Maybe you slept with lanolin glands from freshly slaughtered sheep on your face.

She found all of the stuff Charley had asked for, but he was short on thermal coils, at least in his sock drawer. She didn't really relish poking around in the swamp of his shorts and T-shirt drawer, which seemed like the next logical place to look for them in terms of Charley's unique filing system. She would just pick some up down at Tech City. Imagine a religion founded on desert potholes! What Looney Tune things folks were driven to in the name of religion and quest for spirituality. She supposed she would find out more about it when she went out there. Pahata Ra! And a lavender jet. Well, it was a job, she supposed. Was there that much difference between a spiritual ripoff artist and her private jet and a leveraged-buyout artist and his private jet?

In truth, Calista was not looking forward entirely to this trip. It constituted a major psychological hurdle for her, but it was absolutely mandatory that she surmount it. Almost four years earlier, her husband and Charley's father, Tom Jacobs, the eminent Harvard astrophysicist, had died in the desert of Nevada. A rattlesnake had been placed in his sleeping bag.

Tom Jacobs had been summoned to a paleo-Indian archaeology site to investigate rumors of fraud on the dig. He had invented a remarkable machine known as the Time Slicer that could help in proving such a fraud. It was suspected that the site had been seeded with phoney artifacts. The Time Slicer, a very refined dating instrument with capabilities of determining the provenance of objects through detection of trace elements, had indeed proved the case against a certain Peter Gardiner. It had been Gardiner who had put the snake in Tom's sleeping bag and made sure that there was no anti-venom substance in the camp. A year afterward Gardiner himself had committed suicide.

Archie Baldwin, acting head of the Smithsonian department of archaelogy, had been the first one to suspect Gardiner's fraud and had contacted Tom Jacobs. It was nearly two and half years later that he and Jacobs's widow, Calista, had become lovers. Now she was heading west to the country that had killed her husband and to Archie and her son Charley. She was nervous, damned nervous. But of course, she kept telling herself it had not been the country that had killed Tom. It had been the act of one sick human being. She had always loved that country. It had been Tom's and her favorite place to go trout fishing. They had fished their fair share of the great trout rivers of the West and there had been rattlesnakes as well as trout around those places. They had been careful, of course, but never scared. And she didn't want to be scared now. It had not been the land that caused the problems. She must keep that straight in her mind. Fear was a terrible legacy to pass on to one's child. She had been so pleased when Charley was so enthusiastic about Archie's offer. It was a remarkable achievement for Charley that he had not let those memories cripple his desire to go, to help and contribute to Archie's work. Charley had been the one, after all, who had really taken the bull by the horns, or perhaps the snake by the fangs, and shortly after his father's death had gone and looked up everything he could find in any book on crotalus horridus horridus—more commonly known as the North American rattlesnake.

So when she had kissed them both goodbye at the airport she, who told Charley to be careful when he walked into Harvard Square, had not even said Take care, or Be careful. She didn't want him to think that she was nervous or thinking about it. But of course they were, they all three were thinking about it. They just could not let that kind of irrational fear rule their lives. But Archie crushed his face into her ear as he was kissing her and whispered, "Don't you worry." The words were like rugged little chunks. They did help. And she had needed to have some recognition that this was not altogether a piece of cake for her. But perhaps that was why he could go now, uncrippled and even with enthusiasm.

**4**————————————Calista had decided then to ease her way into the West rather like a swimmer getting into cold water. First she would go to Indianapolis, where her parents lived, and visit them. So Tuesday found her sitting in the beauty shop at L. S. Ayres, a department store in downtown Indianapolis, having a manicure. It was one of her rituals. They gave the best manicures anywhere, including a hot oil treatment, for all of nine dollars. The last of the great bargains. It was a lovely, old-fashioned beauty shop. Women sat under hair dryers—in rollers, no less! No blow-drying here, please. And Lord knew how many cans of hair spray they went through in a day. Of course there was nothing they could do with Calista's hair. It was beyond their wildest nightmares. Thick, unruly, piled on top of her head with a barrette that Charley said looked like an electromagnet, her hair was shot through with silvery gray that she had steadfastly refused to color over the years because coloring represented one more maintenance chore that she simply did not want to keep up. It was too hard to get the color to come out the same every month. Putting paint on hair was not like putting paint on paper—at which she was an expert. Yet even now the colorists circled her like sharks on the scent of fresh blood.

"Did you see Mrs. Van DeVere? I've been doing her for years, Mrs. Jacobs. Her hair has not become porous, because we do a heat cream treatment once a month. So it takes the dye beautifully every time." She pointed to another lady who was sitting with a padded helmet on and looked like a Conehead from "Saturday Night Live."

"But then I'd have to come to Indianapolis once a month for the heat treatments, which really makes it very expensive."

"No, no. We sell these heat caps and the cream. You can do it at home," offered another colorist.

"Too much trouble. I'm into low maintenance. I don't even have grass in my yard, or just a little."

"Whatcha got?" The manicurist looked up. She was applying clear polish to Calista's nails.

"Rocks. They never die."

"Rocks . . ." a colorist said vaguely as if turning over the idea in her mind and trying to imagine such a yard.

"Yeah, beautiful huge boulders, like a Japanese garden. No work."

"Good," said the manicurist. "There's nothing like gardening to mess up your nails."

Calista wondered silently what archaeology would do to hers. She wanted to try digging and scraping and sifting for all of those elusive clues of the past—the fragments of pottery, the arrowhead, or point, as they called it, the inscribed slate, the sliver of worked stone—all the signs that said human life had transpired here, that knowledge had been passed on, that there had stirred in the breasts of these men and women the belief that ideas outlast people and thus culture had been born.

The sites that Archie and his crew were digging were not the paleo-Indian hunter-gatherer sites that showed signs of a transient people following herds or the seasonal cycles of piñon nuts. These hunter-gatherer sites tended to be short-term ones, often male dominated, or, as they said in the abstracts Calista had read, "activity analysis indicating male extraction and fabrication." No girls allowed.

Archie was now focused on the Anasazi sites that had begun in the four-corners area of Utah, New Mexico, Arizona, and Colorado and then spread out. These people, whose name meant basket maker, had not been transients. They had stopped, settled, built, tilled, and created art. They had enough time to think up religion and jewelry and—who knew—sex ed. and aerobics. And they did this high up, on beautiful mesas and plateaus that hung above timber lines, close to the sky. Then they had left, become one of those tantalizing, mysterious disappearances along with the dinosaurs and the Neanderthal people. They had simply vanished for no discernible reason, and their beautiful cliff dwellings were left hanging in the thin pure air.

Calista wanted to see it all. She wanted to touch the delicately inscribed slates, the fragments of earliest pottery, the meticulously tooled beads of some of the first artists of the new world. How thrilling to be the first human eyes in one thousand years or more to see a piece of art—two artists reaching out over a vast gulf of time, the welding together of disparate imaginations.

That evening she sat with her parents in their den. They were playing poker. Her father had just relieved her of five dollars. He was a champion poker player. He had written books on poker playing as well as trout fishing. He got it all together in one book called *Bluffing*. He was doing that to her just now. She could feel it—the eye with the slight astigmatism looking out from under the snarly eyebrow that hiked up antically as he called and lay down three eights.

"Shit," Calista muttered.

"You should have seen what he did the other night—called on a pair of sixes."

"I hate taking money from children," he growled as he raked in the pot and rolled his unlit cigar from one corner of his mouth to the other.

"Ha-ha!" Calista laughed. "Charley told me at Christmas you took him for fifteen bucks."

"Wanted to teach the boy a lesson . . . besides, I gave it back to him at Chanukah. Kid made out like a bandit with that new modess thing."

"Modem, Dad, modem."

"Modess, my dear." Calista's mother, Dorothy, spoke in a low voice. "Modess was a kind of sanitary napkin. I don't even think they make it anymore."

"Modess, modem . . . what the hell."

This was hardly a Norman Rockwell tableau of a family, but despite outward appearances and the truculent chunks of talk that sometimes passed for conversation, they were exceedingly close-knit. Calista's mother was a portrait artist and her father was in the restaurant equipment business. They were somewhat solitary folk, as was Calista, their only child and daughter, and enjoyed the relatively solitary pursuits of trout fishing and poker and painting and drawing.

"I worry about you going out there," Dorothy said suddenly.

"What's there to worry about?" Calista said with almost studied nonchalance. If she could bluff her way through three aces she could certainly handle this. It wasn't quite fair to bring this up in the middle of a poker game. They took their poker seriously. There were rules about such things in the Cohen household.

"Well, you certainly can't have the fondest associations with this desert country," Dorothy said, staring intently at the cards.

"Of course not, but one cannot start blocking out entire sections of the globe."

"You're right, dear." Dorothy looked up and smiled brightly. There was pride in her eyes.

Harry Cohen growled low in his throat, a signal that he was going for a major shift in the conversation, at least in terms of the anxiety level. After all, they had to get back to the business at hand—poker.

"What the hell you say Charley's doin' out there with Archie?" her father asked.

"Ah, figuring out some sort of computer program so they can take all the pottery pieces they find at all the sites and sort them out."

"Oh," grunted Harry. "Good influence, this Archie."

Calista looked at her mother and smiled slightly. They both knew that Harry loved Archie and vice versa, but it was not something that Harry Cohen could quite admit. By using the demonstrative pronoun he distanced himself from this man who was sleeping with his daughter. Old-fashioned, yes. But it was more than that. It was preserving a kind of decorum, a removal that he found essential to conducting life, or at least the parts of it that were important to him—such as poker and trout fishing. This idiosyncrasy had of course spilled over into other areas of his life and had become part of his style. You didn't become cozy or overfamiliar. You must maintain an edge of alertness.

"He still not gettin' bar mitzvahed."

"Who, Archie?" Calista laughed and her mother did to.

"No, bozo, your son?"

"Dad, he's fourteen almost. He's a little late."

"Your Aunt Millie is seventy-five and she just got bas mitz-vahed."

"It's that old geezer she's going with. Didn't you say he's president of the temple or something in Chicago?"

"Yes," said Dorothy. "And Millie never went to services when we were kids. She refused to go even on Yom Kippur and now she's going all the time."

"Shows you what love can do," Calista said.

"And money." Harry was shuffling the cards. Raising his right hand, he dropped them into a perfect parabolic cascade. A movie outfit had once hired Harry, his shuffling hands precisely, to do just this. Very showy, very intimidating to the other players.

"Would you cut the crap, Harry, and just deal," Dorothy said.

"Is he that rich?" Calista asked, taking a sip of the inch of rum her Dad had poured her in between hands.

"Get this, Cookie." Cookie was Harry's pet name for Calista. "He gave himself a stained-glass window at the synagogue."

"Oh come off it, Dad. How do you give yourself a stained-glass window?"

"You just do. You give—what was it that she told us, Dorothy?"

"Fifteen thousand dollars."

"Yeah, fifteen grand and you got the Melvin Slobodkin stained-glass window—have you ever heard of memorializing yourself before you're dead?"

"No," Calista said.

"What hubris," Dorothy offered, picking up her cards and biting her lip thoughtfully.

"Hubris schmoobris." Harry jammed his cigar back in the corner of his mouth.

"That's when Aunt Millie got bas mitzvahed, round the same time as the window installation," Dorothy said.

"I hope he installs some money on her," Calista said.

"I'm not sure she's going to rush into marriage that quick. That Bennie was such a jerk." Until he died "that Bennie" had been Millie's husband for fifty years and Harry's cousin for longer.

"You don't call it rushing when you're seventy-five," Calista said. "How old is Melvin?"

"In his eighties somewhere."

"Well, he's definitely into immortality," Calista said.

"Who isn't, Cookie?" Harry leaned forward and took the cigar out of his mouth. "I just don't want to have to pay for it." He paused, jabbed the cigar in his mouth, and spoke around it. "It's just not kosher."

**5**────────────────── Harry Cohen really didn't like taking money from children, particularly his own. Hence, Calista found herself 36,000 feet over Missouri with a Styrofoam carton of frozen New York strip steaks tucked under the seat in front of her. One of Harry's customers, a local hotel in Indianapolis, had given them to Harry, who in turn had pressed them upon Calista "to make up for what I took from you last night" he said as she climbed into their vintage 1960 Cadillac Eldorado.

Harry had always liked Cadillacs, but old ones. He scoured acres of used-car landscapes for pre-1965 Cadillacs. Calista knew that Harry would press some sort of foodstuff on her. He always did. So she had come with a minimum of carry-on luggage. It was something in the genes of their family. They never traveled without bringing gifts of food. They got off planes with shopping bags stained with the blood of roast beefs and tenderloins. They carried portable vats of matzoh-ball soups and tote bags full of rugelach, smoked salmon, and flash-frozen homemade blintzes. Calista looked now at the Styrofoam case and wondered what kind of cooking facilities Archie had at this camp. She supposed they didn't need much. A grill? Then she nearly laughed out loud. Boy, would that look stupid—a grill set up in the desert. She supposed they wouldn't need charcoal either. After all, wasn't this the place? The source for mesquite, coin of the grilling realm.

If you couldn't find mesquite in Arizona you were in real trouble. No more picking it up for twenty bucks a baglet at one of the fancy yuppie food emporiums in Cambridge or Boston. Next to the Styrofoam case was a rolled canvas affair that looked like a mini-sleeping bag. It wasn't. It was her portable art studio. All the equipment she needed for drawing and watercolor work. In her suitcase was her main sketchbook. It wouldn't roll. Archie had other art supplies out there and she had promised him that she would do any archaeological drawings that he wanted done. Most sites did have an artist to draw the artifacts. It was a very technical kind of drawing, but Calista had done it before, not in the field but when the artifacts were brought back to the labs and museums. It was a different discipline entirely from that of illustrating children's books. She enjoyed it, however. It was a nice break. The plane would be landing in twenty minutes.

As they taxied to the gate Calista noticed on the tarmac far from the main terminal a jet glistening in a most stunning array of colors, the likes of which she had never seen painted on a plane—not even Braniff at its most fanciful. "A mother-of-pearl plane!" she muttered. The hostess was just passing by and noticed her looking at the plane.

"Oh, you're looking at Pahata Ra's jet," she said.

"Pahata Ra?" The name did sound familiar.

"Spiritual leader of the Pahatties—welcome to Arizona Center of New Age Religions. That's Pahata's private jet. She has two, actually. The other one is more of a lavender. The airstrip isn't built yet up at Red Forks so she has to take one of her copters in."

"Oh my God!" whispered Calista. Of course! It was the woman Charley had told her about. She thought about the Time Slicer in her suitcase and all those capacitors, resistors, diodes, and the Hall Effect sensor or whatever the hell it was! This was the pothole religion—yin yang, ling-ling (no, that was the panda at the Washington zoo!). This was the one where God spoke, or rather, his vibes came out of earth holes. A bar mitzvah at seventy-five was starting to have its appeal.

She looked around for Archie and Charley at the gate, but they were nowhere in sight. So she proceeded to the baggage claim area. Just as the escalator slid to the bottom she spotted Archie coming through the door. He saw her, grinned, and jogged toward her. They were hugging. The three weeks apart melted away. It was Archie all right, with a touch of sagebrush clinging to his clothes. If it weren't for the Dos Equis T-shirt and the Red Sox cap he could have been in a Ralph Lauren ad. He wore vintage cowboy boots that he had had resoled countless times and in which he had tramped over every major paleo-Indian site in the Desert West, faded jeans, and gray hair that stuck out, now slightly longish for him, from under his cap. His face was as tanned as an Indian's, his eyes as blue as the sky, and they looked worried.

"Where's Charley?"

"In the car fending off the traffic cops."

"You look tired. What's wrong?"

Archie laughed and squeezed her rear end discreetly. "You look great and, gee, am I glad to see you."

She let him hug her some more and then stood back. "Are you sure nothing's wrong?"

"Well, a kind of problem, but don't worry. Doesn't concern you. I'll tell you about it in the car."

"So Tonk just disappeared without a trace?" Calista asked as they drove out the airport exit onto the highway.

"Not exactly without a trace," Charley said. "His burro wandered into Red Forks last evening."

Calista was squeezed into the front seat of the pickup between Archie and Charley. The back of the pickup was loaded with provisions, which consisted mainly of fifty-gallon drums of water, two butane tanks for the camp's gas-operated refrigerator, and assorted bulk grocery supplies.

"But they've been hunting?" she asked.

"Yeah, but so far nothing. One problem is nobody's quite sure which way the burro wandered into town from. It just kind of appeared down by the old pump, which is in the center of things. So it was hard to figure out where to start. And then, well, people are worried because it seems that Tonk has had a medical problem recently. He was on medication for something called T.I.A."

"T.I.A.?" Calista asked. "What's that?

"Transient Ischemic Amnesia." Archie pushed his aviator glasses up and rubbed one very tired-looking eye. "It's like little strokes that result in temporary memory loss and disorientation. They aren't really all that serious, I guess, and can be controlled by medication, but for a guy Tonk's age and out in the desert, very possibly without his medication, it could be real bad."

"But, Archie," Charley said, "you did say that the burro didn't have any canteens on him. So that's a good sign, isn't it?"

"What do you mean, a good sign?" Calista asked.

"Well," Archie said, "it just means that the burro doesn't have the water, so possibly Tonk has it. But then again, the burro could have had it tied to the pack and it just came loose. In which case nobody's got it and there's an eighty-nine-year-old man out in the desert with no water, and I don't mean just for taking his pills."

"You know this Tonk well?" There she went, being just like her dad with the demonstrative pronoun, trying to distance herself.

"Yeah," Archie replied quietly. "Really well." He paused. "Tonk knew this country better than anyone. Any Desert West archaeologist worth his salt consulted with Tonk on a more regular basis than, say, their thesis adviser, and it got them a damn stretch further."

"What was he?" Calista asked.

"A cowboy." He paused. "Once upon a time a rancher. Most recently mayor of Red Forks."

"Mayor of Red Forks?"

"Yeah, I actually think that they were thinking of putting him in the *Guinness Book of World Records* for most consecutive terms of any mayor. I think he's been mayor since long before World War II."

Charley whistled low. "He came from Montana originally. Legend has it that he rode with Charlie Russell."

"God, he couldn't be that old, could he?" Calista asked.

"No. Russell did his cowboy thing in the 1880s. That was before Tonk's time. Not long, though. Tonk did know him, however, and when he was wrangling up in the Judith Basin area of Montana, which was Russell's stomping ground, Russell would come up to sketch. So you figure Tonk has made it into a fair share of Russell's paintings as a kind of live action model?" Archie paused again and sighed. "I just hope to God he's still live action."

"Yeah," Charley interjected. "And he was your main hope for dealing with the Rainbow Coalition."

"The Rainbow Coalition?"

"It's not Jesse Jackson," said Archie.

"That's just what Archie and me and the folks at camp call it."

"They are very partial to rainbows."

"And holes in the ground," Charley added. "Not exactly holes."

"No they are implied holes, to be precise," Archie added and then paused. "But nothing is very precise in this religion."

"You brought the Time Slicer, didn't you, Mom?"

"Yes."

"See, we're going to help them get a little more precise."

"Charley, I don't think you should go interfering in other people's religion; religious tolerance, you know."

"Don't worry, Mom."

"Yeah, don't worry, Mom." Archie patted her knee. "It just seems that one of the faithful is getting fed up."

"Bored more than fed up, Archie. And Amy was never really one of the faithful either."

"Amy—who's Amy?"

"She's this girl," Charley said.

"*This* girl. You're sounding like your grandfather, Charley. I assumed she was a girl."

"Oh, you shouldn't assume that, Cal." Archie had taken off

his cap and pushed his glasses up on his forehead. His eyes twinkled in the rearview mirror. "Remember the Johnny Cash song—'A Boy Named Sue.' "

"Okay, this girl named Amy."

"You want to know what her other name is?" Charley asked.

"You mean her last name?"

"No, I mean the one they gave her in her naming ceremony."

"What?"

"Her true vibrant monadic resonator?"

"*Whaaat?*"

"Rainbow Da," Charley said flatly.

"What? That's her name?"

"That is her magnetically derived true name."

"What do magnets have to do with it?"

"Not much really," Charley said. "These folks don't know a magnet from a meadow muffin but they are always talking about energy fields and magnetic forces. You know how in the Christian religion they have a lot with wine and Triscuits."

"Wine and Triscuits?" Archie asked, somewhat perplexed.

"Yeah, I mean you're a Christian, Archie."

"Sort of."

"Didn't you do that stuff?"

"If you mean communion, that's mostly for high Episcopalians and Catholics, which I wasn't. And I don't think it was Triscuits."

"Well, I want to know what magnets have to do with all this, and who is Amy Rainbow what's-her-name?"

"I'm just saying that magnetic fields are to these people a kind of theme."

"A motif of sorts, if you will," Archie interjected.

"Thanks, Arch. Yeah, the way the wine and the crackers or whatever are to high Episcopalians and Catholics."

"You mean it's symbolic," Calista said.

"No!" Archie and Charley both answered at once.

"That's just the problem. It's not symbolic to them. They believe in this as a kind of science—divine science. They can't tell the difference between symbols and real things," Archie said.

"And what's really bad is that they don't know anything about magnetic fields or magnetism," Charley added.

"So now tell me about Amy, whose name has been magnetically determined."

"She's cute," Charley said.

Calista and Archie exchanged glances in the rearview mirror. This was the first public admittance that Charley had ever made of his susceptibility or attraction to the opposite sex. He had carefully watched from the bench as a few of his more daring classmates had ventured out onto the court for their first dates.

It didn't take long to tell the short, very simple story of Amy and her mother and stepfather, who had become followers of Pahata Ra. They, along with several hundreds of other followers, had followed the ancient spirit who traveled in mother-of-pearl jets and lavender helicopters to Red Forks, Arizona, and founded Rancho Radiance.

"I wish to hell they'd just pack up their rainbows and skedaddle," Archie muttered.

"You mean they actually won't let you dig?"

"They haven't said absolutely no. But they're talking permits, stuff like that. I've got Bureau of Land Management permits up the wazoo. And that would have done me fine until a month ago. You gotta understand that out here the amount of state-owned, federally-owned and privately owned land is constantly changing—almost daily."

"But you've been digging for the last three weeks."

"Sure, up at Horse Creek and Devil's Canyon. But we were just finishing up those sites really. We've spent the last week backfilling."

"Backfilling? What's that?" Calista asked.

"Filling in the dirt you've taken out. Restoring the site to the point at which you found it—unless, of course, it's a pueblo. You don't want to cover up the city you just uncovered. But the pits, all that, have to be restored. Now it's time to move on to the Los Gatos site. There is a great cliff dwelling, but there's

other stuff too. We dug the test trenches last summer. It's the
focus of our work, or should be for the next five field seasons.
It's rich." Archie clamped his mouth together and then blew out
some air. "God, is it rich. There is just so much there that we
could tie in with the spread of the Anasazi culture to the Mogollon. They seemed to take over the Mogollon so quickly.
Overshadowed them completely by, say, A.D. 900, but this is
where the shadow didn't drop so completely, eclipse entirely. It's
a real telescope of a site, or I guess I should say a periscope—
because if we can dig it we can really look around a corner that
for a long time has been a blind one. We had our permits and
everything."

"And then?" Calista asked.

"Dum de dum dum," Charley intoned.

"Enter Pahata Ra," Archie said and slid his glasses back down
as they turned west from the big highway to a smaller road.

"She bought it."

"As of three weeks ago the papers were passed. It's no longer
under BLM control. Now, most of these private landholders kind
of like having us around. . . ." He let the sentence trail off.

"But not Pahata Ra?"

"Well, again she hasn't said she doesn't like us. In a very
carefully worded letter she has said she has the greatest respect
for our work, for she feels it is part of a spectrum of increasing
understanding and appreciation for the world of the ancients,
and of course as the chief honcho and major PR person for ancient
spirits—you know she claims to be sixty-five thousand years
old. . . ."

"Yeah, so what's the problem? She should love you."

"The problem is the holes, or vortices, as they call them. They
are afraid that my holes will disturb their holes."

"The implied ones in the ground or the ones in their head?"
Calista said. Charley and Archie both laughed at this.

"Probably both," Archie said, and gave Calista's knee a
squeeze.

"So what kind of permit do you have to get?"

"I'm not even sure, to tell you the truth, because before out here the ranchers always have been so nice about it. I just ask permission, write a letter of intent, get it notarized, and that's it. But now they're talking county regulatory agency permits and easements . . . and oh, Jesus!"

"Or oh, Pahata Ra!" Charley said.

"Yes, precisely. It's very hard when God moves to town and starts investing in real estate."

"Who the hell is she?" Calista asked.

"Who knows. She sounds fairly articulate when she speaks— not smart, but I mean educated, or at least a patina of education. I haven't really seen her in person. Just on some videotapes they played at a town meeting. But once you get through the robes and the beatific glaze on her face, I don't know, I'd say she's just basically your girl next door—slight New Jersey accent—maybe Jewish."

"Oh dear."

"Maybe Italian."

"Mafia?"

"Now, Calista, that is not nice. The Anti-Defamation League'll get after you on that one."

"Sorry."

They turned onto a dirt road. A long-eared jackrabbit sprinted out from behind a saguaro cactus, and two magpies darted and dived in the sky that hung like a bright blue wedge between two red rock spires. Just before a cattle grate in the road was a hand-lettered sign:

**Welcome to West Red Forks, Smithsonian Field Station. Big kahuna Archie Baldwin, asst. kahuna Ted Moran. Elves: Susie, Charley, Tom, Jenny, Elsbeth, Holly, Mike, Brian. Cook: Stevie Child (absolutely no relation to Julia).**

Below the names was more writing:

**Las Vegas 200 miles, nearest grocery 92.8 mi., Harvard Square 2,788.2 mi. Ascension Island 7,542 mi. Disneyland 535.1. Best lay (m. or f.) 95.3 mi. and 101.8 mi. respectively.**

Archie stopped the car and Charley hopped out to open the gate. They drove through. Archie stopped again. Charley closed the gate and climbed back in. Fifty feet down the road was another sign.

**Have you hugged your screening box today?**

Another fifty feet another sign:

**This is your safe sex stop.**

A paper cup labeled CONDOMS was taped to the sign.
"Gee, this crew really has a sense of humor," Calista said.
"He made them take down one." Charley giggled.
"What was that one?" Calista asked.
"Something about a rainbow with a hard-on," Archie growled. "Best left unsaid, specially while we're trying to get permission to dig."

**6**————————A billow of bright orange and green silk-like cloth floated over the top of the hard ground. It was attached at four points by thin guy lines. Underneath were card tables and what appeared to be file cabinets.
"My father's spinnaker makes a great lab tent," Archie said as

they pulled up. "He blew it out in the last Bermuda race, but I got it stitched up and it really makes a fine place to work."

Scattered in a loose circumference around the lab tent were smaller sleeping tents.

"What's that?" Calista said, pointing toward a bright white triangular awning.

"Oh, that's the cook tent—Chez Stevie, we call it. Also a relic from one of Dad's boats. I think it was a mizzen staysail."

Archie's father, Will, was a renowned singlehanded sailor and at the age of seventy-one had been the oldest man to win the transatlantic sailing race. His sails blew out before he did. At the age of eighty he was still sailing vigorously. "And that, my dear," said Archie, pointing beyond Chez Stevie, "is our love nest."

"Where?" Calista asked.

"That over there." He pointed to a large tent.

"It's the biggest tent after the lab tent and Chez Stevie."

"I know, didn't you see the sign? I'm the big kahuna. When you're my age and still going out on digs you get the biggest tent—that's part of the deal." He paused and smiled at Calista. "I could tell you the joke about the rainbow with the hard-on and why we need the biggest tent."

"Archie!" Calista's neck flared red. When she blushed it was not just in her face. In a paroxysm of capillary action red streaks raked down her entire neck. Archie loved to watch her blush. She looked around for Charley. He had already slipped out of the truck and had joined some team workers who seemed to be playing a game beyond the cook tent.

"I can't wait to you-know-what." Archie rippled his hand through the air.

"Me neither, but it's broad daylight and if we go into that tent—even though I do notice you have placed it at a discreet distance from the rest—people might think that we're . . ." She clamped her lips shut. Her eyes sparkled, and she tossed her head back and forth. "Doing it."

"I bet they would."

"Especially when I scream in orgasmic delight and the tent

blows out like that spinnaker in the Bermuda race. It wouldn't be nice. I bet all these kids are horny as hell what with the nearest lay being, what is it, ninety-five point three miles away."

"Well, nearest—best, whatever. It is for everybody except Brian and Susie. Theirs is about thirty feet. They've taken up. We can do it in the dark, though, if we stuff socks in our mouths. I washed them just for the occasion."

"You nut." Calista punched him in the shoulder.

A tall young man with lanky yellow hair came out from the lab tent.

"Hi, Brian."

"Hi, Arch."

"This is Calista, Charley's mom. What's up? Any sign of Tonk?"

"Not that we've heard. Tom and Susie and Jenny and Mike went off to join the search. Apparently the Pahatties have joined in too."

"That's nice of them. Where'd you hear that, from Amy?"

"She's here?"

Calista raised an eyebrow. "Yeah," Brian continued. "Her mother dropped her off. She thought Charley would be here and he was teaching her some sort of programming thing."

"Gee, I'd like to meet Amy," Calista said.

"Well, I guess you will," said Archie.

"I was going back into town later to pick up the rest of the crew and, uh, see if they've made any progress in deciding if we can dig at Los Gastos—Swami Ben-ji Prem La is going to bring it up at the town council meeting."

"What?" Archie said.

"You didn't know, Arch, that Swami Ben-ji is the new president of the city council?"

"I didn't even know they had a city council. I knew there was a county regulatory agency, or whatever they call it."

"Of course they have a city council, and Tonk is on it along with a selectman or two and Ben-ji is on it because, after all, Rancho Radiance is one of the most densely populated areas of the township now and it wasn't hard for him to win with a constituency like that. He's been on the town council since last November. They're having a meeting at four this afternoon. I thought someone should go. I wasn't sure you'd be back in time."

"Well, I'll definitely go," Archie said. "But I still don't understand, if this is private property, why we have to go through this kind of red tape. Why can't we just meet with the Rancho Radiance people and do this directly? I'd really like to take them out to Devil's Creek and Greasy Canyon and show them how nicely we've backfilled those areas, restored them perfectly."

"Well, that was my idea too," Brian said. "We might as well give it a try."

"When are you going?"

" 'Bout half an hour. I promised Amy's mom that we'd drop her in town so they can pick her up there."

"Okay. Want to go, Calista?"

"Sure."

"I don't understand it," Calista said. They were back in the truck. This time it was Archie, Calista, and Brian in the cab. Charley and Amy were riding in the back of the pickup with two other kids from the dig.

"You don't understand what?"

"She is so adorable and she obviously loves being around all you folks. Why would any parent drag their kid out here to pay homage to some guru? She's very lively and was so excited about the computer stuff Charley was teaching her."

"Yeah," said Brian. "You should hear her go on about those seminars and meditation sessions she has to attend. The poor kid is bored out of her mind."

Calista glimpsed Amy through the rearview mirror. She had a wonderful face—round, a nicely dimpled chin, and big apple cheeks. Her eyes were a lovely liquid brown and fringed with very dark lashes, although her hair was a much lighter color—almost blond. Her eyes were long rather than round, which gave them a dramatic look. And when she smiled, as she was now doing, they crinkled up merrily and sparkled.

"What's that?" asked Calista, pointing to a structure a quarter mile or more off the road.

"A hogan—one of the few in this area. This is a nice one, though a polygonal one. I bet it's been twenty years since it's been used for a curing ceremony."

"That's on Claudia Perkins's land, though, isn't it?" Brian asked.

"Believe so. Hey, she must be upset about Tonk."

"Wherever she is," Brian said.

"What do you mean, wherever she is? Isn't she around?"

"Apparently she went off to visit some relatives over in Yuma or maybe New Mexico."

"Claudia did?" Archie asked.

"Yeah? Why?"

"Do you know Claudia?"

"I met her last year just once, I think," Brian answered.

"Well, she wasn't the type to go off visiting relatives. She goes off all right—all the time. She'll just take a hike."

"Archie, at eighty-five or whatever she just hikes off?"

"Yeah, she always has. But she's pretty much of a recluse and I can't imagine her going to visit relatives."

"Huh," said Brian.

"She would have been a good one to have gone out looking for Tonk."

"At eighty-five?" Calista said.

"Yeah, she knew the terrain and she knew Tonk's ways. They had been pretty tight in the past."

Archie slammed on the brakes and the truck screeched to a halt. "What the fuck?" He pointed at the sign ahead. It was a city-limits sign for Red Forks announcing the population, but just beyond the old city-limits sign was another sign.

**Pahata Ra welcomes you to Red Forks.**

"My God, they've even got a historical marker, now how did they wangle that out of the county?" Archie pulled the car up closer. "Gotta read the fine print on this one." They were just a few feet now from the historical marker.

"Red Forks, Arizona is not only a place of awesome beauty,"

Archie began reading,

"but extraordinary energy. It is considered by psychic pilgrims—

What the heck are psychic pilgrims?"
"Not you, I think, Archie," Calista said. Brian laughed.
"Okay," Archie continued.

"It is considered by psychic pilgrims to be a power spot and as such one of the four places from which great concentrations of positive energy are emitted from the earth. The Red Forks area has more vortices for emissions of these positive energy particles than any other place on earth. We welcome you and all psychic pilgrims to this magnificent area of transcendent beauty and spiritualism in the name of Pahata Ra, ancient spirit from a previous world. We hope that in quiet contemplation on the rim of the many vortices in this region you too shall gain a feeling of new vitality and attunement to your previous lives and experiences. We ask that you please respect the landscape and do not defile by physically or spiritually littering. Remember negative spiritual vibrations are every bit as destructive as paper. Go in peace and harmony."

Archie turned away from the sign toward Brian and Calista. "How the fuck did she have the gall and get the permission to put this marker up?" Amy was now tapping on the glass window between the back of the pickup and the cab, her brown eyes twinkling.

"What, Amy?" Archie said through the glass.

"She owns the land!"

"She does?" Archie's eyes opened wide.

"Yeah. Wait a minute," Amy shouted. A few seconds later she was leaning around the edge of the pickup on the driver's side. Her bright, dimpled face peered into the window. "Note that the sign is a few yards within that stone marker, not right on the town line. That's the southwest corner of Rancho Radiance, the new parcel they just got."

"And I guess she can put up any kind of sign she wants to on her own property."

"You got it, Archie," Amy said, and pulled back from the window.

"I've got to meet this lady!" Calista said.

"Fat chance," Brian replied.

"Why?"

"She doesn't cotton to outsiders that much. It's real hard getting in there. Security is tight."

"Has Amy met her?"

"Oh yeah. I think Amy's mother is one of the big donors. She's got access, as they say."

7
—————————————— Red Forks, depending on your perspective, Calista thought, appeared to be a town either en route to oblivion, or partway back from it—a kind of half ghost town. But which way it was going was anybody's guess. It straggled out of a twisted canyon, basically a one-street town, and only one side of that one street was really built up at all. The buildings had an air of being framed up for the most part from

bits and pieces lying around loose from other towns. The most imposing building in town was the white frame Red Forks Hotel with its turquoise-blue trim and shutters. The hotel was now called the Psychic Pilgrim Inn, but the outline of the old name, which had been removed from the pediment over the door, hovered like a restless spirit. A paint crew was just setting up to complete the job of eradication. And to all intents and purposes it looked as if they were planning to paint a rainbow over the old name.

Archie stopped the car and got out. He looked up at the pediment where the paint crew was putting up the ladders. " 'Nother rainbow?" he asked a young fellow with a wispy beard.

"You bet," the man answered cheerfully.

A girl with a ring in her nose and a very small rainbow drawn on her cheek turned and said, "The restaurant's open now."

"Was it ever closed?" Archie asked.

"Oh yes. We've switched over to a totally vegetarian menu and we had to go through a ritual cleansing."

"Oh," said Archie.

"Is the Palatki Bar still open?"

"It's a juice bar now and it's called the Power Spot."

"The what?"

"The Power Spot," the girl repeated, and smiled broadly. The little rainbow on her cheek took a hike toward her eye when she smiled.

"What was wrong with the name Palatki?"

"Nothing, I guess," the girl answered, "but you know Red Forks is one of the four great power spots of the world and we figured it should be recognized."

Archie shook his head, whistled low, and chuckled.

"You're laughing." The rainbow dropped down a quarter inch.

"Not really. I just think it's kind of ironic. I mean Red Forks has had an odd history in a sense. The Sinagua moved on because it was too damn dry for them. The Mormons avoided it. Back in the twenties people got all excited because some turquoise was discovered up around Devil's Creek and there was great anticipation that Red Forks might become a turquoise boom town. But it petered out after about the first week and a half. They found maybe all of twenty turquoises. Then, when they were gerrymandering county borders around like crazy, Red Forks was the one that nobody really wanted. It's always fallen between the cracks or just out of the reach for federal or state assistance programs. People are forever arguing about who has the responsibility for Red Forks. It's like the eternal foster child. It just seems funny now to hear it called a Power Spot. That is the last thing that anyone would ever think to call Red Forks." He shook his head again then looked up at the girl questioningly. "You know, I really like that name Palatki."

"Well, as I said, there wasn't anything wrong with it."

"No, that's just the point. It was just right, perfect. You know what the word means?"

"No."

"It means red. It's the Hopi word for red. *Palatkwabi* is the Hopi word for red land." Archie looked up at the steep wall of the canyon that embraced the town. "That's all you see around here red—red rocks, red soil, and Palatki is such a nice-sounding word."

The girl leaned forward slightly. Her large breasts swung like pendulous melons under the thin Indian print shirt. Calista wondered if she had rainbows painted on them too. "But did you know that there is more than just red rocks here?"

"Yeah," said Archie flatly. Calista could not tell whether that response was a question or a statement.

The girl's voice dropped. "There is a huge crystal deep underneath Red Forks, buried way down. Once there was a city there, the city of Zemira."

"Oh," said Archie quietly. He did not sneer. There was not a trace of scoff in his voice, Calista thought. Perhaps just a little pity in his eyes. Good Lord, he could be tolerant!

They walked on toward what passed for the town hall. "So," muttered Archie, "Sedona's got the tourism, the other three counties have the water, for the most part, every other town has something cute that has made it a historical landmark or is a genuine ghost town with an Indian trading post or souvenir shop, and what does Red Forks have—a fucking crystal buried underneath it so every New Age crackpot can come and contemplate their navels, or whatever it is they do, which doesn't add up to much more than spiritual masturbation."

"Am I supposed to say 'Now, now, dear,' or what?"

" 'Or what,' say that. Oh, look," Archie said, nodding ahead. "Guess Amy's found her mother."

*"Borrrring."* The word reverberated as it rolled out of Amy's mouth. The mother and daughter were standing just in front of the town hall, a crumbling building of red sandstone with an elaborate parapet over the entrance that seemed in better shape than the rest of the building. Amy had her head turned away. Her eyes were glazed over and the lively face that Calista had seen in the rearview mirror had a dead, ashen appearance. Amy did not even seem to register Calista's presence as she and Archie approached. She and her mother both turned and walked toward a jeep across the street. The mother wore tight designer jeans and a white T-shirt. She appeared to be in her late thirties. She walked uncomfortably in her shiny new cowboy boots and the discomfort made her appear to prance rather than actually walk. She had a good figure.

"She stays in shape," Archie said. "Spiritually, I was meaning."

"Yeah, I bet." Calista laughed. "She's wearing a push-up bra."

"A push-up bra?"

"You know, like all those eighteenth-century maidens. It makes you look like you have twice as much and it increases the jiggle quotient."

"The jiggle quotient?"

"More bounce to the ounce."

"And you can tell from here that she's wearing one of those."

"Yep. Remember, I'm an artist! An astute observer of the human form and even sometimes behavior, and what I am observing now is that she is not paying a bit of attention to her sulking daughter but is aiming those jiggling boobies toward that guy who's leaning against the jeep with the rainbow painted on its door."

A tall man with shoulder-length black hair and a plaited head-band of turquoise and silver was almost reclining across the hood of the jeep. He looked as if he were working on his tan, which was easy to do, as he was wearing a leather vest with no shirt on underneath it.

They were now in front of the town hall.

A plump, sixtyish woman came out of the front door. "No sign," she said. She wore a star on her gingham blouse. Her straight black hair was pulled back into a stubby club of a ponytail. The heavy-lidded eyes behind the bifocals betrayed no expression. Annie Fuentes was of Scottish-Navajo descent, and she was the sheriff of the town of Red Forks. "We've had people out looking since his burro came in."

"Nothing?"

"Nothing," she said dully. "I don't know, Archie. I don't think it looks too hopeful. He's on medication for those seizures. Who knows if he had the stuff with him or not. Getting dehydrated out there'd be enough to bring one on, and he does get dis-oriented. He came down to the clinic day before yesterday and Dr. Jackson was fussing with the dosage and going to try out something new. I actually was supposed to go over and take his blood pressure twice a day." In addition to being the sheriff of Red Forks, Annie was an LPN and worked in the clinic in Wins-low three days a week. "You going into the meeting?"

"Yeah. This is my friend Calista Jacobs."

"You Charley's mom?"

"Yes."

"He's a nice kid. Real smart. That rainbow gal, she likes being with him more than with her own family. Don't blame her. She ain't learning anything from them silly Pahatties. Charley's teach-ing her a lot. I let them hook up one of those computers in the sheriff's office." Then she paused and laughed. "He said he could

get me one of them whatchamacallits—modems—and hook me
up with the sheriffs in other counties." She shook her head and
laughed deeply. "Sheriffs in other counties don't want to talk to
me. Always trouble when Red Forks calls up, ain't it, Archie?"

"Yeah, like now. Aren't you going into the meeting, Annie?"

"S'pose I should. But it's so stupid. They sit there with a
goddam crystal in the middle of the table and ask for unity or
something and good vibrations, and what's the first motion but
to change the name of the town."

"What?" Archie almost barked.

"Yeah, they want to change the name—to something Crystal
City or, I don't know, Rainbow Ridge. Ain't no ridge. We're
stuck in this canyon. Claudie Perkins like to die. After all, her
folks was the ones who named it, I think."

"Where is Claudie?"

"Beats me. They say she's down in Yuma. She sent somebody
a postcard. I don't know. You know Claudie. But I don't worry
about Claudie. She takes off all the time—walking or riding. She
can hike fifty, sixty miles over the roughest stuff and never show
it. She's as healthy as a horse. And she's ornery and a loner. So
you really can't worry 'bout folk like that. But I'm plenty worried
about Tonk." She paused and looked straight out into the town.
A slight smile played across her face. "You know what Tonk
called these Pahatties with their crystals and all?"

"No what's that?" Archie asked.

"Born Again Crystals!" They all laughed. "God, I miss him."
Annie sighed and twisted the toe of her leather boot into the red
dirt of the street.


# 8 ———————————— Calista and Archie had taken

seats in the back of the room, although it was hardly necessary,
as the room was less than packed. Six people sat around a

rectangular table. Ten to fifteen other people were in folding chairs facing the table. A plump, bald man with thick-rimmed glasses and a saffron-colored shirt of thin cotton held the gavel. He was obviously conducting the meeting. In the middle of the table there rested a large amethyst-colored quartz. A rather desiccated little lady in a flowered shirtwaist dress and a hairnet, the kind waitresses used to wear, would occasionally steal a glance at the quartz. For the most part, however, she kept her eyes riveted on a stenographer's notebook in which she was writing. Calista guesssed that she was perhaps the secretary and keeping the minutes of the meeting. She was obviously not comfortable with the situation. "That's Agnes Bessie. I think she's the town clerk," Archie whispered. "And the one next to her has something to do with zoning. The others are selectmen and -women, I guess, although they hardly look as if they are from the area."

"Hardly," Calista whispered back. Of the three other people at the table, two had tiny rainbows drawn on either their cheeks or foreheads and all wore some kind of crystal jewelry—earrings, bracelets, or necklaces. One of the men leaned across to a woman with an abundance of curly red hair and whispered something. She nodded in a friendly, conciliatory way and removed a necklace which she put in her pocketbook.

"Tourmaline interference," the man said.

Some of the older and more obviously longtime locals shifted slightly in their seats and exchanged nervous glances. Agnes Bessie stopped writing in her notebook and looked up directly at the plump, bald man.

"Do I write that in the minutes?"

"What?" The fat man's eyes blinked behind the thick lenses of his glasses.

"The stuff about tourmaline interference."

"I don't think it's necessary, Ms. Bessie."

"It's Mrs. Bessie," she replied curtly.

"Agnes?" an old man at the end of the table spoke up.

"What is it, Coy?"

"Did you bring the Congo bars?"

"The Congo bars?" asked the lady of the tourmaline necklace. Her tone was one of complete bewilderment. In all, there were six people around the table—Agnes Bessie, Coy McSparrow, and Lucille Greyeyes were the obvious longtime locals. The other three were dwellers of Rancho Radiance and newly elected to the town council.

"Agnes always makes Congo bars for town council," Coy growled. "She has since she's been on. How long has that been, Aggie?"

"Thirty-five years." She was holding the tin box rather nervously in her hands and glacing at the quartz.

"For Crissake, pass it on down here. Congo bars ain't going to interfere with any rock. If a rock gets spooked by a Congo bar it ain't no rock." Coy laughed a toothless cackle. "Pass 'em on down here."

Agnes removed the lid and folded back the tin foil. She passed the box to the man on her left, who wore his hair in Apache-style braids. In his right nostril he wore an ameythst stud. Agnes could not help staring at it and visibly winced as she passed him the tin box. He turned toward her.

"Do these have any animal fats in them?" he asked.

Agnes's mouth moved, but no words came out immediately. It was like a film out of sync by a frame. The words finally formed. But she never took her eyes off the jeweled nostril.

"No, of course not. They're cookies, or cake-cookies. Don't use animals—just margarine," she replied.

"Pass 'em on down here, young fella," Coy urged. "Take one. They haven't killed anyone yet."

The members of the council each took one. Agnes turned to the people sitting in the audience. "I'm sorry I didn't make enough for you folks. You caught me short. Usually nobody shows up at town meetin'."

"Don't worry none, Aggie . . . now . . . now . . . we'll bring our own. You don't have to go feedin' the whole town," various voices replied.

Coy had taken a wide-mouth quart glass jar from a satchel by his feet.

"You brought your own iced tea, Mr. McSparrow?" the fat man said. The room suddenly convulsed in laughter.

"Tea?" Coy chuckled.

"It's not tea?" the fat man asked.

"Noooo," said Coy, sliding his eyes toward the fat man. A wicked merriment glinted in the faded old eyes.

"What, may I ask then, are you drinking?"

"Whiskey."

Giggles scattered like birdshot through the room.

The fat man sighed deeply and ran his hands over his jaw. Who was that guy? Calista thought. That fat face—there was something familiar about it. Or did all fat bald men look alike—like Buddha or Telly Savalas, or a combination thereof?

"Do you allow this?" he asked somberly with rather deliberate incredulity.

"What do you mean, 'allow'?" Lucille Greyeyes spoke in her soft, accented Navajo cadences. "Coy's been around longer than anybody except Tonk, Mr. Prem La."

"Oh," said the fat man quietly. But there was an uneasiness, and Calista felt that this would not be the last word on the subject. "By the way, Mrs. Greyeyes," he continued. "Most people do not call me Mr. Prem La. My full name is Swami Ben-ji Prem La and most people just call me Swami Ben or perhaps Swami Ben-ji. If you feel more comfortable with Mr. Prem La, fine. But it has a rather formal ring to it and I am not a particularly formal kind of person."

Just "divine," thought Calista, not formal.

Now it was Lucille Greyeyes's turn to say "Oh," which she did, although Calista had the feeling that she would prefer not to use any form of address from here on. At this point Coy pulled out a smaller jar, a jelly jar, set it down hard on the table, and poured two inches of the whiskey into it while glaring defiantly at Swami Ben-ji Prem La. Swami Ben-ji returned the look with a cold stare.

"So much for that hunk of quartz providing harmony," Archie whispered.

"As first councilman and acting head now of the town council because of the absence of Mayor Tonk Cullen," Prem La began, "I would like to suggest that our first order of business here should be a report on the search heretofore undertaken for Mr. Cullen and how we might plan to continue it."

"Smart," whispered Archie. "Politically very smart."

"Mr. McSparrow, I believe you've been instrumental in planning the search, being so familair with the region."

Lucille Greyeyes and Agnes Bessie exchanged glances. There was a shadow of embarrassment in their eyes. Calista picked it up immediately. How odd and completely out of kilter for a stranger to come into town, somehow get elected to the council, and then tell Coy McSparrow, who had lived in Red Forks over sixty years, that he, Coy, was familiar with the territory. Coy gave his report succinctly, summing up the territory that the search had covered so far—Canyon Diablo, the north and the south rim. And where it was going—West Fork of Chili Bean Creek up to Tonto Wash.

The next item on the agenda was the motion to allocate funds for restoration of the old jail, which in the entire history of Red Forks had been occupied by only three criminals. It had functioned briefly as a school when there were schoolchildren, but, alas, all the children had grown up and the people of childbearing age had moved toward Flagstaff or down toward Winslow. So, for lack of criminals or kids, the old adobe structure had fallen into disrepair. It had been considered by many to be a very classic example of adobe architecture, and Agnes Bessie, who lived next door to the jail and was head of the Red Forks Historical Society, had long entertained notions of a third incarnation of the old jail—that of museum. But her pen now stopped scratching the minutes in her precise minuscule handwriting.

"What?" she whispered, and blinked. Lucille Greyeyes's hand reached out and touched Agnes's softly.

"I said that I think we should postpone any discussion of

allocating any funds, since the building is right now up for sale," Prem La said.

"But how can it be up for sale?" Agnes answered, bewildered.

"It belonged to a certain Lottie Farraday," he was saying.

"Lottie Farraday died forty years ago," Lucille said.

"Yes," answered Prem La. "And her heirs, the last of whom died five years ago, hadn't paid taxes for fifteen years. So it is going to be up for auction. The papers are to be filed with the county. You folks have been a tad neglectful about little details like these."

"How does he know that the last heir died five years ago?" Calista whispered.

"Good question," replied Archie. "Pretty arcane piece of information to come up with."

"Are there any interested buyers?" Lucille asked.

"Yes," answered the woman who had worn the tourmaline necklace. "I'm quite interested."

"What do you want a jail for?" Coy asked.

The woman sat up a little straighter. "Mr. McSparrow, I am a certified rebirther and herbalist. I am also a facilitator in past life regression therapy."

"What's she talkin' about?" Coy said, turning to the audience.

There was a nervous twitter. Coy turned back. "What does this have to do with buyin' the jail?"

"I want to open up a holistic life guidance multidimensional counseling center."

"In the jail?" Agnes Bessie said weakly.

"Yes," the woman replied.

"Perhaps, Miss Kaye," Lucille Greyeyes began in a friendly voice but in a tone of great forbearance, "you could explain to us about rebirthing and this other business."

Miss Kaye seemed to wince slightly at the word "business." "Rebirthing is a process"—her voice rang out crisply—"through which an individual is literally drawn back to a birth experience."

"Why would anyone want to do that?" Coy blurted out. The

audience roared, and even Lucille Greyeyes, who had been a model of polite attentiveness, ducked her chin to her chest and smiled. Agnes just looked confused.

"Agnes is taking this hard," Archie said. "She has always nurtured a dream of a real museum here in Red Forks."

Andrea Kaye was now explaining past life regression therapy and the use of crystals in facilitating the journey. Coy seemed to be listening attentively. He poured himself another inch of whiskey.

"You mean to say, miss, if I put one of these here rocks on my head . . ."

"A meteorite piece or Herkimer diamond is preferable."

"Diamond—that'll be hard to come by, but just supposin' I kin get one. If I put it on I might darn well discover I'm Zane Grey."

"Coy," a voice from the audience shouted, "you can't be Zane Grey. He only died sixty years ago. You and him were living at the same time."

"By Jesus, you're right, Sam. I plumb forgot. I saw him down at Payson once't."

"Well, you're smart, Coy, but you ain't that smart to live two lives at one time."

The room erupted in laughter, and Coy laughed too, his shoulders heaving up and down as he lifted the glass of whiskey to his grizzled face.

"The next item on our agenda," Prem La began, "is the request by Dr. Archibald Baldwin." There was a slight rustle in the audience. Nobody ever called Archie Archibald, and it sounded funny to hear him referred to that way. "The request is for permission to dig a site that is now in the southeast quadrant of Rancho Radiance, we having recently acquired that parcel of land that extends down to Los Gatos Wash. There is apparently an interesting paleo-Indian site there."

"Not apparently, Mr. Prem La. It is there. I first found it three summers ago when the land was still federally owned and under the Bureau of Land Management. Last year, when it became state owned, I dug several trenches that revealed paleo-Indian occupation—a Mogollon site."

"Yes, well . . ." Mr. Prem La began.

"Well, what's the problem?" Coy asked. "Archie's dug all over here for years. He always gits the permits if it's a BLM deal and if it's private we just say aw go 'head. It's the closest we ever git to bein' in the Smithsonian."

"Yes." Lucille and Agnes both nodded. Then Lucille added, "It's an honor we have all enjoyed. You say it's Mogollon, Archie?" She pronounced the word as Muggy Owen. "I never knew they got up this far."

"Neither did we. But it has all the indications. That's what makes it so exciting."

"Mogollon. I'll be," Lucille said softly.

The Mogollon peoples developed a sedentary lifestyle several hundred years earlier than the famed Anasazis, who were renowned for their exquisite pueblo dwellings. So although the Anasazis were considered the acme in many respects in terms of the culture they developed it had become clear that the tradition had had its roots in another people—the Mogollon. But Mogollon sites were rare and sites that showed the overlap between the Anasazis and the Mogollon people were virtually nonexistent—until Los Gatos. It was important to understand this site; it was crucial to a better understanding not only of the ancient pueblo desert dwellers but of vital questions about transmission of culture in general. But now this fat man was saying no.

"It is against the precepts of Rancho Radiance to disturb these ancient sites. If you read the teachings of Pahata Ra, you will better understand that it is our belief that there is a Transcendental Bridge that is in fact an evolutionary path to God and a higher state of consciousness. We believe that this bridge in that it is both subjective and objective is emblematic of the basic physics of the universe. It is composed of both matter and energy. As one moves across the bridge one travels from dense states to freer states, gaining a wider range of perception."

"What in tarnation does this have to do with Archie digging?" Coy asked.

"Took the words right out of my mouth, Coy," Archie said.

"Try some of this." Coy raised his glass and nodded toward Archie. "You'd talk a little faster." The audience laughed. Prem La frowned. He obviously did not enjoy being upstaged by this whiskey-swilling old codger.

"It has quite a bit to do with it, Mr. McSparrow. We believe that the bridge begins at Rancho Radiance. You can call it a bridge, or a thread, or whatever. But this path has its origins near the site of these ancient peoples. They knew the way. The energy centers are very well organized, articulated into a number of vortices, or power spots, which emanate high levels of positive energy. The ancients knew it and we know it. We feel it is not judicious to go probing and fiddling with the earth in these regions."

"I don't fiddle," Archie said rather grimly.

"Yes, I know, and although you have explained on previous occasions that you go to great pains upon finishing an excavation to restore it as closely as possible to the condition in which you originally found it through backfilling techniques, you still must admit that a disturbance has occurred, would you not, Dr. Baldwin?"

"Of course, but you yourselves at Rancho Radiance have erected numerous buildings—I think fifteen at latest count. Wouldn't you say that this disturbs too?"

"I am afraid I am not following you, sir. There were no paleo-Indian sites on any of the places where we have built our buildings and we were careful to put only our meditation huts near vortices."

As opposed to toilets, kitchens, or hot tubs, Calista thought. This guy was too much. They were all too much and it did not look promising for Archie.

"Well, I seriously doubt if our excavations of this site would in any way interfere with the path or Rainbow Bridge that you have so"—he coughed—"so clearly delineated for us. But if you say that indeed the ancient people were quite tuned in to this bridge it would seem to me that any further understanding of these people could only enhance your understanding of their cosmos and in turn benefit you." It was an artful and graceful little speech and indeed it seemed to move the two other new members of the council. It was smart of Archie to use the word cosmos.

The young fellow with the Apache braids spoke up. "Swami, I don't think there would be any harm in our at least bringing up this issue with Pahata Ra when she gets back."

Andrea Kaye nodded her head in agreement. "It's true if we can better understand their cosmos, their mode of perception as they experienced this land, well, perhaps . . . you know that's a point."

Prem La's face remained placid. Deceptively placid, Calista thought. He was not about to have an open disagreement with his own troops in front of all these people. No way. But he was smart and very powerful. She could feel it. And, God, that face was familiar. It would haunt her until she could place it.

"All right, we shall discuss it when Pahata returns. I would suggest, however, in the meantime that Dr. Baldwin be aware of the fact that the documents he now has, the permits from the BLM, are null and void in reference to this land and that he must proceed through the proper channels. For whether his request is granted or not he must make proper application. I believe that is done through the regulatory board in Flagstaff."

Bureaucracy was always a last refuge for small minds. Annie Fuentes had entered the room about halfway through the meeting. Her hand now went up.

"Yes, Sheriff. Do you have a question?"

"I missed the first part of the meeting, so maybe you already discussed this, but what about the name change?"

There was a low murmur. "What name change?" Lucille asked.

"Oh, you haven't discussed it?" Annie said, all innocence.

"That was not on the agenda for this meeting, Sheriff, and I would appreciate it if . . ."

"What name change, Mr. Prem La?" Lucille asked very distinctly, with a sharp edge to her voice.

"Why you sly fox, you!" Archie said, turning around and winking at Annie. She had spilled the beans before they were ready, caught them off guard. A superb tactic. Obviously she had overheard them talking about this name change, but they had had no intention of bringing it up until they were good and ready, which was not now.

"There had been some discussion about changing the name of Red Forks."

"What?" There was a chorus of disgruntled voices and some angry rumblings.

"Where had such discussion taken place, Mr. Prem La?" Lucille Greyeyes asked.

"Oh, nothing formal, mind you."

"Of course not. If I may remind you, the town council operates here under a set of bylaws, and before there can be any formal discussions the topic must be submitted to the secretary and put on an agenda at least three weeks in advance of the meeting unless it is deemed an emergency, and this isn't."

Archie was flabbergasted. He had never seen Lucille Greyeyes angry, but she was now. She leaned forward. "Red Forks has been Red Forks since Claudie Perkins's family founded it. They named it, and if there's any changing to be done, well, Claudie should at least have a say."

Prem La had been watching Lucille with his usual placid expression, but now his eyes jerked nervously away. Archie and Calista both noticed it. Something had upset him more than even Apache Braids and Miss Tourmaline's suggestion that they take up Archie's request with Pahata.

Andrea Kaye then turned to Lucille and in her sweetest voice, the kind nurses use when they are telling a child that it won't hurt, said, "Well, Ms. Greyeyes, we were just kicking around some ideas for names that we thought would be more reflective."

Lucille was actually rising in her seat now as if mesmerized by the transgression suggested. "Miss Kaye, you can kick it around elsewhere. It's not on the agenda. There will be no further discussion."

"I second the motion," Coy said, raising his glass.

Prem La was just about to say that a motion had not been made. But Agnes Bessie did an end run around him. "I move that there will be no further discussion for any name change of Red Forks without Claudie Perkins present."

"I second it again," Coy said.

Prem La actually looked a little dazed as he was caught in the crossfire of these manipulations of Robert's Rules of Order. The meeting adjourned almost immediately.

# 9

"'Use Inner Beauty to enhance dull and boring food. Keep away from pets, open flames, unsupervised children, and bad advice. This is not a toy. This is serious. Stand up straight, sit right, and stop mumbling.' Got that, folks?" Charley looked up.

He was reading from the label of the bottle of Inner Beauty hot sauce, which proclaimed itself the hottest sauce in North America. It came direct from the East Coast Grill, one of Calista and Charley's favorite restaurants in Cambridge, Massachusetts. It was about to be pitted against "Roast Guts—Pancho Villa's Favorite." The steaks Calista had brought from Indianapolis were sizzling on the grill.

"Cocktail time. Want a petrone, Calista?" Ted Moran, the most senior of the graduate students and listed as assistant kahuna to Archie on the signpost, came up with a plastic pitcher containing some ominous-colored fluid.

"Dare I ask? What's a petrone?"

"Oh, Calista! Don't embarrass me like this." Archie looked up from the portable field table where, with the aid of a Coleman lantern, he was examining some pottery fragments.

"She's your lady friend"—Brian looked up—"and doesn't know what a petrone is?"

This was the first time any of these kids, many of whom had worked with Archie for several field seasons throughout their graduate and undergraduate years, had ever seen him with a woman. They seemed to enjoy it. There had always been talk that he had had lady friends, but he had gone to great lengths to keep that part of his life separate from his work, in the field at least. The students were secretly relieved when they met Calista. They had never expected anyone so approachable. They liked seeing their leader in love. Of course Archie Baldwin was anything but demonstrative in front of them, but in the short time—a matter of hours—that she had been at the camp, they could still tell. It was the way they caught him looking at her and laughing at her jokes.

"So what's a petrone?" she asked again.

"The desert drink, my dear. Vodka and Gatorade," Archie answered.

"Well, I guess I'll give it a try." Ted poured her a plastic cup. She took a sip. Everyone waited. It was absolutely ghastly—sweet and fruity. The vodka did little to cut it. She swallowed.

"It's an acquired taste," Archie offered.

"I guess so. Can we add something to it?"

"Like what?"

"Vermouth instead of Gatorade?"

"No, no! You've gotta have the Gatorade."

"Why?"

"Keeps your electrolytes up in this heat."

"What does the vodka do?"

"Makes you forget about your electrolytes altogether."

"Oh." She paused and tried another sip. She kept her eyes riveted directly ahead on a canyon wall that was caught in the purple shadows of the descending night. The sun had set nearly forty-five minutes earlier, but in its afterglow sharkish clouds raced against a bruised sky over the rough terrain. There would be lots to paint out here. "How come you call these things pe-trones?" she asked.

"Derivative more or less of petroglyphs—those rocks inscribed with pictures."

"Uh-oh! I gather that this is to suggest that one must have a stonelike gut for the inscriptions of this drink."

"Anybody who can take Inner Beauty hot sauce will have no problems with a petrone."

"Who's that dude with the vest and the hairy chest that Amy's mom was with, Charley?" Calista asked.

"David Many Hearts."

"David Who?" Calista asked and took another sip of her drink. She looked up, startled. "I can't believe this. I actually am ac-quiring a taste for these things."

"It's your electrolytes—see, you must have been drained," said Archie. "If you respond this well we might fill your canteen tomorrow with desperadoes."

"What are desperadoes?"

"Bloody Marys made with Gatorade. Perfect for a hangover."

"Oh. Anyhow, who is David Many Whats?"

"He runs the self-actualization workshops at Rancho Radi-ance," Charley said.

"The what?" Archie looked up from the fragment of pottery.

"I don't know what it is. Self-actualization. Amy says it's real boring. But her mother thinks it's great and is always making her go. And she says that David Many Hearts is a total jerk. But her mother thinks that he's great too. And this really bugs Amy, and Ralph especially."

"Who's Ralph? God, I need a libretto to follow all this."

"Ralph is Amy's stepfather. He's pretty nice. But he looks just like Mister Rogers."

"Oh dear," Calista said, "I can't imagine subjecting a child to this sort of thing. Not Mister Rogers, the rest of it.

"I know," said Charley. "And she's the oldest kid there. All the others are really little. But her mother's easing up on making her go to all these workshops and stuff. She's been real nice about letting her help me with the computer programming. She seems to think it's worthwhile, if not self-actualizing. They're always talking like that. And the food they eat is just gross—all these grains and things. God, she was so grateful to Archie when she went into Phoenix with him time before last and he drove her straight to a McDonald's for a Big Mac."

"I felt sorry for her. It was the least I could do. Speaking of which, are those steaks ready yet, Steve?"

"One more minute for those who like them rare."

By the time they sat down at the picnic table to eat a chill breeze had begun to blow and the temperature had dropped a quick fifteen degrees. They were bundled up in sweatshirts and lightweight parkas. Archie lit candles on the table that sat in coffee tins half filled with sand and punched with nail holes. He liked such niceties for camp life. And each day someone was dispatched to gather some flowers or wild grasses. Tonight there was some larkspur and columbine sharing an old Skippy peanut butter jar. The desert versions of these flowers seemed lighter, more delicate. They were not precisely in the desert zone, however. Holly Addison had climbed to some high country that was strictly speaking in the transition zone, an elevation of 6,500 feet between Upper Sonoran, where the camp was, and the Canadian zone, to gather these flowers.

Holly was the chief documenter of rock art and often went into the higher elevations where there were old hunting shelters, caves, and rock overhangs that had a wealth of pictographs as well as petroglyphs. The talk at the table was more subdued than usual, for as night had fallen and the cold wind blew down across the land, there was not one person who was not thinking of Tonk Cullen—alone out there in this high desert country.

In addition to being the recorder of rock art, Holly was also the premier marksperson with a sling.

"Time for fun and games at Camp Baldwin," she announced after the dinner dishes had been cleaned up.

"Oh no!" Archie groaned, getting out his pipe. "Time for the Harvard Smithsonian Invitational Pro Am, eh?"

Playtime at any archaeological camp involves attempting to acquire certain skills of ancient people. It is all part of the hands-on analysis of those people's technology. Every department of archaeology and anthropology has some young graduate student who has become an expert flintknapper. One cannot study, hold, or examine the lithic designs of prehistoric people without becoming tempted by the challenge of turning a rock into a blade, a point, or a chopper. Charley himself, in the year and a half since Archie had entered his and his mother's lives, had become fairly adept at flintknapping. His challenge now was the sling, not a slingshot. The difference between the two was that a sling relied on centrifugal action as opposed to spring action. It was much harder to master but could attain greater accuracy and force. Holly had become the master of the leather pouch sling. She could knock a Band-Aid box off a post at a distance of one hundred feet. She had also become proficient in what she called the double-whammy technique, which involved firing off two stones in rapid succession. Ths was exceedingly difficult and required a great deal of rhythm and fluid motion. It was what Charley was working on now.

Charley, Ted, Brian, and Holly walked off toward the target range, which was beyond the latrines. They started with single shots. It had taken Charley a full two weeks to get that down. The hardest part in the beginning of learning to work a sling was simply to get the thing whirling without letting the stone drop out. The idea was to build up enough momentum of centrifugal force to keep the stone in the pouch until it was to be released. Then all that force had to hurl it like a missile toward the target. So for the first week Charley could not even keep the darn stone in the pouch. It kept dropping out. The second week it stayed in and he began working on his accuracy. He was hitting three out of five by the end of the week. Now he wanted to learn the double whammy. He tried a couple of times and felt unbelievably clumsy. He was back at square one, with stones dropping out all over the place.

"You're thinking too hard, Charley. Don't think about the second stone at all until your arm is in the down swing of the arc. Then catch the sling and put the stone in the pouch while it's still moving."

She demonstrated. It was all one fluid movement. The sling did not appear to stop at all when she loaded it with the second stone.

After dinner, while the kids practiced with their slings, Calista and Archie took a walk. "We're a little late," Archie said.

"Late for what?" Calista asked. They were on top of a mesa and he had his arm around her shoulders.

"The sunset. I like to walk up here at sunset every night. You know the Hopis have a belief that at the end of the day, after all the work is done, a person should stand in the doorway of his house and let the rays of the setting sun wash over him, wash out all the weariness of the day. I usually come up here every evening at sunset. I like to think of this particular view and this mesa as a doorway. I like it better than any doorway I've ever owned."

It was a spectacular view. The darkness had quenched the crimson fire of the land and the stars had just started to break out. The wind-torn rocks rose now like herds of fantastic beasts in dark profiles against the night. The yips of a coyote suddenly punctuated the stillness of the evening. It was a land of dream, of myth.

But why, why, Calista thought, couldn't these people at Rancho Radiance with their dime-store visions, which amounted to no more than a bad mishmash of cultures, keep quiet? Why must they proselytize and display their beliefs like gaudy costumes? With all their gibberish about power spots and rainbow bridges they had managed to reduce thousands of years of mystical culture to a carnival. The New Age! It was becoming a spiritual midway. Great for the sacramental thrill seekers! There you could ride the transcendental loop-the-loop and the Rainbow Roller Coaster to greater awareness and go to the side shows presided over by carny barkers now called gurus—those merchants of inner bliss.

"I know you're having very profound thoughts," Archie said in a soft, husky voice.

"What makes you think that?"

"It's the way you chew on your lower lip."

"Okay." She laughed gently and stopped chewing on her lip.

"The problem is . . ." He paused. She turned her face up toward him. He was holding her from behind with both his arms around her.

"What's the problem?"

"I am having less profound thoughts."

"Oh?"

"Yeah, like I'm horny as hell for you and how 'bout you let me jump your bones?"

"Right here?"

"No. In honor of this occasion I purchased the L. L. Bean double sleeping bag with Quallofil and self-inflating Therm-a-Rest foam pads—two of them. They hook together. Isn't that romantic?"

Charley had kept practicing the double whammy until the light was too poor, and then he kept on because he figured he couldn't hit a target if he saw it anyway. So he just kept trying to launch his missiles into the night. The stars were so brilliant. He could never help but think of his dad on a night like this. Everything that he knew about the sky, about the universe, about the new astronomy, as it was called, and the old he had learned from his dad. And for all the knowledge, all the theories, all the great minds from Ptolemy to Galileo from Kepler to Einstein and Hawking, the most impressive thing Charley thought, no not thought, felt, as he flung his head back and launched a stone into the black dome of the night was this: I am in the desert of a very small planet of a minor galaxy, a little speck with a teeny, tiny weapon—what a joke! And he laughed at the night and thought that his dad might laugh too.

Archie had pitched the tent away from the others. This was always his habit as much to protect his privacy as theirs. He had no desire to know who was slipping into whose tent on these digs. Although life on a dig was a communal affair with so much shared and so little privacy, there was still an undeniable romance to any expedition in this high desert country. This was the case whether romance actually took place or not. However, if it did, people should be able to take full advantage of the intrinsic beauty of the land. Part of this beauty was its emptiness, its loneliness, its timelessness: within the immensity of the land to be in a small tent, wrapped in somebody's arms within a cocoon of darkness, to feel someone's heart beating against one's own, someone who rocked within one's body in acts of love, was to be momentarily found in a limitless universe. They made love far into that bound- less night.

Not long before dawn Calista awoke. Through the tent flap she could see that the blackness of the night had thinned and the last of the night's stars hung in that fragile gray light before the dawn, as ironic as a single jewel against a Quaker lady's dress. She felt Archie wake up next to her.

"You awake, Cal?"

"Yes." His hand snuggled over and cupped her breast. She yawned. "I have to pee and it's so far to the latrine in this cold."

"You can go out in the sagebrush." Now she was embarrassed to tell him, but she really had to go. "Archie . . ."

"Yeah?"

"I'm scared of the dark and . . ." she paused.

"And you're scared of rattlesnakes," he added and pulled her close to him. Archie Baldwin had been the one to request that Tom Jacobs go to the desert in the first place, and although he had subsequently fallen in love with Calista he had never met her until a year later. Still, he would never get over having inadvertently been instrumental in sending Jacobs on his last trip, which had had such a tragic conclusion. "Well, what if I walk out there with you and ride shotgun, so to speak?"

"Well, it's kind of embarrassing peeing in front of you."

"I'll try not to look, but wouldn't it be more embarrassing if you peed in our brand-new L. L. Bean double sleeping bag?" Calista began to giggle. "Oh, for Crissake, Calista, don't start laughing—you really might!"

They grabbed some clothes and their parkas and lurched out of the tent. A hundred yards away they found the perfect clump of sagebrush. Archie began poking at it vigorously with a walking stick he often carried with him when hiking.

> *Hickory Dickory Dock,*
> he recited,
> *the mouse ran up the clock*
> *The clock struck one and down he run*
> *Hickory Dickory Dock.*

"Archie, what are you doing?"

"Letting them know we're here. Okay, I don't think there are any snakes around, at least not in that clump. Fire away. I'll turn my back."

Calista squatted. "Gads, I hope I'm not doing this on a vortex."

"Calista, I can't watch out for everything. Would you please just pee."

She giggled. "But, Archie, what if it's a power spot?"

"I could say something very lascivious here, but I won't."

"Like 'Peter, Peter, Pumpkin eater . . .' "

"Calista!" Archie began laughing now. "Would you just shut up and pee!"

"All right."

**10**_____They sat with their legs dangling over a sheer cliff, facing east, and drank their coffee silently as they looked across the valley floor below toward the Castle Rocks a mile or more away. The gray veil of dawn was just lifting and a rose tint began to brush over the rocks. In another hour they would be the color of poppies. Sun was the oxygen of the rock's blood. It pumped a red life into them. To sit on this rim of the world and witness their resuscitation was an amazing drama of transformation. A wind blew down across the valley, bringing with it the scent of juniper mingled with that of sagebrush. There was a prayerfulness about the land at this hour. But it was a land of natural rituals without need for priests, dogma, or symbols. The land itself had become the liturgy and the house of worship. The rest—the incense, the candles or crystals, the churches, cathedrals, or synagogues, the chanting—were all pale imitations of what was occurring and had been occurring every morning for four billion years.

Archie's hand rested lightly on her knee as she drank in these colors, these forms. It would be another half hour before the camp was up.

"I want to join the search for Tonk today." Archie spoke quietly. "And I want to go up to Claudie's place."

"Why's that?" Calista asked.

"I want to see how she left it. I know she goes off all the time, but she's been gone a long time now, longer than usual. She kept a couple of goats and things. I just want to see how she arranged for this long an absence."

She didn't, was the answer. The first sound they heard as they approached Claudie Perkins's house was the whine of a gate swinging in the breeze. Under an escarpment was Claudie's "barnyard." The fencing extended out from the base of the sheer face of the cliff. The overhang offered some protection for the few animals she kept. There was also a shed backing up to the base of the cliff for shelter in the most inclement weather. This was not an uncommon arrangement. An escarpment such as this one lessened the construction work and provided natural insulating features for animals. Easy to keep the coyotes out and the domestic animals in. Except now there were no animals in.

Claudie's house was a low square house made of red sandstone blocks with a wooden roof. It was a style prevalent in the early part of the century and was known as Anglo, although it was widely used among the Navajo. A cow skull rested at the foot of the path leading up to the front door over which a pair of antlers was nailed. There had been an attempt to grow some petunias in pots, but they appeared to have shriveled up and died. Archie stood in front of one of these pots now and scratched his head. "This isn't right. Claudie never let her petunias just go to hell like this."

"I would have thought watering them would have been a problem," Calista said.

"Not for Claudie. She owned the Red Forks water company, for one thing."

"She owned a water company? I've never heard of such a thing."

"Out here it's common. There are a lot of privately owned water companies. They have to answer, of course, to the state water commission and adhere to certain regulations, but they are still privately owned. Anyhow, let's go in and take a look around."

"The mice have had a field day," Calista said, standing in the middle of the kitchen. There was a bowl of withered apples and rock-hard lemons in the middle of a table covered with a blue checkered cloth. Except for the mouse droppings the house appeared immaculate. Wicks were trimmed in kerosene lamps, pillows neatly propped on a daybed. It was a house of simple shapes and simple materials. There were earthen jugs and wooden bowls, Navajo rugs and faded old patchwork quilts.

Archie was in the bedroom when he called out, "Cal, how many suitcase do you suppose a woman like Claudie might own?"

"I don't know for sure, but one would seem like a good guess."

"That's what I thought too. And guess what? It's here."

"And not in Yuma," Calista added.

"Right. I suppose we can't call that conclusive evidence."

"Yeah," said Calista as he walked out of the bedroom. "But how 'bout this?"

"What?"

She held out a dustpan toward him. "Look, I found this right here in the kitchen. It was filled with sweepings. Why would a person as neat as Claudie appears to be not empty her dustpan?"

"It doesn't make sense, does it?" Archie said.

"No. Even if you were caught short on time, you'd always have time to just dump this in the trash. Look, here's the trash can not two feet away."

"You'd always have time unless you were interrupted."

"Permanently interrupted?" Calista whispered softly.

"I don't like the looks of this," Archie said, rubbing his chin. "I don't quite know where to begin, but you know, I think that Tonk maybe didn't like the looks of this either."

"You think he went off hunting for Claudie?"

"Possibly."

They walked around Claudie's spread for another forty-five minutes. "Well, her pickup's definitely not here, nor is her horse," Archie said. "That, including her feet, are the A to Z of Claudie's modes of transport. So it does look as if she's gone somewhere even if she didn't take her suitcase." They walked around to the back of the house to the kitchen garden. Melon vines withered in the summer sun, carrot tops had shriveled, and runner beans had collapsed entirely on their string guidelines. The garden had not been watered in weeks. Archie shook his head again. "She would have arranged for someone to come up and water this stuff." He paused. "I think we've got two missing old people, not just one."

. . .

By five-thirty that afternoon the search parties had returned with no word on Tonk. Soon a decision would have to be made as to whether or not to continue the search on their own or get assistance from the state. Prem La's generous offer of the Pahata's second helicopter and pilot had been taken up that afternoon, and for the better part of four hours the staccato sounds of the chopper could be heard scouring the sky over the rugged canyon lands. So it was doubtful whether additional assistance would actually help that much more, since an aerial search had so far yielded nothing.

"You say this is her handwriting, Agnes?" Archie stood in Agnes Bessie's kitchen and looked at a postcard.

Agnes nodded. "I can't understand, though, why she wouldn't have arranged for anybody to go up there and water her garden and the pots. That's not like Claudie. But this is definitely her writing. You know she always handwrites out those bills from the water company, or she did until Annie started taking them down to some secretarial service in Winslow. And you know one never did pry with Claudie. If she said she was going off, you just didn't ask why." She paused, then turned to Calista. "She was a most private person." She shook her head. "You say it was all cleaned up up there."

"Yes." Archie nodded.

"She was a very tidy person. So she would leave things very neat if she were leaving on a long trip."

Calista thought of the dustpan with the sweepings but did not mention it. It was clear that Agnes Bessie was deeply concerned over Claudie's absence, and she had not been prepared for the fact that it might be anything other than one of Claudie's usual little sojourns.

"Well, I don't want to alarm you, but it just occurred to me that perhaps Tonk was concerned about her and went out looking," Archie said.

"Yes, yes. He would be." Agnes looked up, and her eyes had a faraway look in them. "Tonk, if anyone, would be very concerned." A shadow swept across her faded hazel eyes, which suddenly seemed ineffably sad to Calista.

"Right now I wouldn't say too much about this. After all, we don't know anything really for sure."

"Just that she didn't water her garden." Agnes laughed almost bitterly. "No, you're right, Archie. No sense gettin' everyone in an uproar."

"I'll talk to Annie about trying to track down her relatives or whereabouts in Yuma."

"This here postcard don't give much information." Agnes picked it up and looked at it and read it aloud in a very soft voice. " 'Dear Agnes, It's hotter here than in Red Forks. Awful lot of people. I'll bring you back a souvenir. Yours, Claudie.' "

At least, thought Calista, she didn't say "wish you were here." She was beginning to have the most dreadful feelings about Claudia Perkins.

# 11

———————————— "Okay," Charley was saying, "you say that this is a vortex here. I guess I should have guessed from the stone ring around it."

"Absolutely. It's the one they took me to when they renamed me." Amy nodded. "This is a positively charged vortex and its vibrational frequency yielded my true monadic resonance—in other words my name—Rainbow Da. This, of course, is a yin one, a feminine one, magnetically."

"I never did get the connection between the girl thing and the magnetic thing—it's not part of any physics that I'm familiar with," Charley said.

"Well, do you think your machine will still work?"

"Sure. It doesn't know a girl from a boy, a horse from a cow. But it's very sensitive in other respects, like the tiny little variations in magnetic alignment."

"What does that mean?" Amy asked.

"In rocks, in dirt there can be trace elements—iron, zinc, magnesium, stuff like that. Okay, so it can detect the presence of those elements, but that's still no big deal. What it really does is show variations. See, you know how over time the magnetic poles have shifted?"

"No, I didn't know that. And they're talking all the time about magnetism and frequencies and vibrations—especially David Many Hearts."

"Well, there's nothing very subtle about it. It was figured out a while ago through potassium-argon dating. You can see exactly when there have been reversals in the geomagnetic field— changes in polarities. My dad's machine, the Time Slicer, does the same thing, except in a much more refined way. Where potassium-argon dating deals in epochs and eras—you know, chunks of millions of years—the Time Slicer can just slice the geological pie thinner—thousand-year chunks, or I guess slivers. I could read in a very refined way what they call magnetic noise and get quite a bit of information out of these readings. You can even get geomagnetic latitudes out of this baby," Charley said, affectionately patting the machine, which was not much bigger than a blow-dryer.

"And what does that mean?" Amy asked, pushing back her thick hair from her brow.

"It means that you can figure out where a particular rock came from originally, if by chance it has moved."

"But we don't have to know if anything's been moved here. We just want to figure out if . . ." she paused.

"If these power spots have any magnetic qualities." Charley finished her thought.

"Can it do that?"

"Of course. It's baby stuff for the Time Slicer. We're not trying to determine where anything is coming from or even the dating stuff. We're just trying to see if all this so-called vibrational energy is really there."

"And giving my name!" Amy giggled.

"Now that might stretch the Slicer's capacities to actually come up with a name for a person, but it can tell us if this place has the super energy that they are claiming it has."

"David says that when you enter the vibrational field of a vortex you can feel your consciousness expanding. I couldn't feel anything, and unfortunately I said so. Boy, was my mom pissed when I said that." She blushed furiously when she remembered precisely what her mother had said. All sorts of stuff about being such an angry child, being anally retentive—that was the worst.

Charley opened a fresh set of batteries and put them into the Time Slicer. He then replaced some of the old diodes with some of the new ones his mother had brought him from Cambridge.

"What are you doing now?" Amy asked.

"Just making sure everything is fresh—fully charged batteries, new diodes. We want this thing working up to speed." From another small zippered leather bag he took out something that looked similar to a telephone-answering machine.

"And what's that?"

"Little Ozo thermal printer."

"What do you need that for?"

Charley looked up and widened his eyes. "Recording our results. We can't just fly in there and say there is or there isn't a concentration of energy—we saw it with our own eyes, take it on faith! No way, Jose. This gives us the recorded proof—the evidence. See, I just hit the button and it will print out the data from the Time Slicer—as soon as I wire them together."

"Gee, Charley, you're really smart about these things."

"I'm not smart at all. Haven't you taken any science courses?"

"Sure."

"Well, you know those lab books they give you or lab worksheets where they have those headings—Inquiry, Hypothesis, Observational Data, Conclusions—and you fill in the blanks?"

"Sure. But I just never thought of this as being the same thing."

"It is the same thing—we're using the same procedure. We're

just not doing it in a lab. The hypothesis here is that there is a concentration of energy and that this particular place has—what do they call it?"

"Yin."

"Yin energy, which they equate to the magnetic energy of a vibrational field."

"It is also supposed to have some yang—which makes it perfectly balanced, like an electromagnet."

"What do they mean 'balanced like an electromagnet'? I never heard of electromagnets talked about in terms of balance and I've messed with a lot of them."

"Don't ask me, Charley." Amy shrugged her shoulders.

"Anyhow, the hypothesis is that there is an electromagnetic energy here that is special, concentrated in some way that has impact on human systems."

"Yeah, I guess that about sums up what they say. Although I have my doubts."

"Well, science proceeds by doubt, not faith. So we are here as doubters and we have to set up an experiment to first assess if there is any extra energy here at all. If there is, we then have to try and figure out how it works to affect any living thing at all— especially humans."

Amy's brow furrowed. "Why do you say 'especially humans'?"

Charley was busy screwing in the last wire lead to the Ozo printer from the Time Slicer. "Because living things are not really magnetic systems per se."

"What do you mean by that?"

"Well, I should say people are not, as compared to pigeons."

"Pigeons?" Amy asked, bewildered.

"Yeah. If you had to say that any animal had a slightly magnetic orientation you might say pigeons and I guess dolphins too maybe. You ever watch 'Nova'?"

"You mean that television program?"

"Yeah. They had this show on once and these guys up at Cornell were trying to figure out stuff about pigeon navigational systems. These birds can usually find their way home no matter what. It's just incredible. They put frosted contact lenses on them so they couldn't see and they could still fly home; they put them through all sorts of disorienting maneuvers but they always found their way home with no trouble. The only thing that they did that mixed them up just a little bit and only temporarily was when they strapped small magnets to their heads. This in fact did screw up their navigation for a while. But what they realized was that pilots had reported radio transmission problems in this area too. It has to do with variations in the magnetic field. So around Ithaca, New York, there were such variations and a pigeon brain, which they discovered had something like a little built-in compass and was magnetically sensitive, could be messed up if a magnet were put on its head. But people basically are not magnetized systems. We don't have brains anything like pigeons', so a magnetic field with some anomalies in it is not going to affect us really—at least not like a pigeon."

"Oh," Amy said. "That makes pretty much sense."

She was watching Charley clasp a needle with a pair of small alligator clips. "What are you doing now?"

"This is the sensor. I'm just going to stick this right in the center of the vortex and we'll see what it comes up with. Now where's the center, or rather, where did you get your magnetically inspired name?"

"Right about there." Amy leaned over and pointed to a place about eighteen inches away. They were both on their knees.

"Okay, here we go," Charley said. He pushed the sensor into the ground and flipped the Time Slicer's switch. The needle did a limp little jiggle and then sagged.

"Looks like Cleveland to me," he said.

"But it moved, Charley!" Amy said excitedly.

"But it would have moved in Cleveland too. It's just picking up on the trace magnetic noise. The whole earth, after all, is a magnet. This is just the normal stuff. I've got a data base back at the computer in camp. If there's enough juice tonight back there and Archie will let me run it I can show you how this reading compares to a mess of other places."

"So there's no exceptional concentration of energy here?"

"Nope, but we'll get a printout just to show it, and we can walk around and stick the sensor in other places nearby that are not supposed to be power spots and see how it compares."

Within a half an hour they had twenty other readouts, all with identical magnetic noise profiles and no indication of any excessive electrical energy of any kind—yin, yang, or anything else.

"What about crystals?" Amy asked.

"What about them?"

"Could they have an effect?"

Charley was bewildered. "How?"

"Well, you know, crystal therapy."

"Crystal therapy? I've never heard of it."

"Andrea, that lady with the red hair, is supposed to be a big-deal crystal therapist. She's going to open a clinic in town and she was at my naming ceremony and when they did it they gave me a yellow crystal to hold." She paused and dug into her jeans pocket. "I got it right here. I'm supposed to carry it at all times." She drew out a slender pale yellow crystal.

Charley stared down at it. "And what's that supposed to do?"

"I don't know . . . open me to some sort of deeper energy source within myself, heal me."

"Of what?"

"Of . . . of . . . " She shrugged, then blushed. "Of not getting along with my mom, I think." And she laughed. "You know they believe in all this stuff. They say that crystals have this special energy. Andrea lays them on people's bodies and cures them of all sorts of things."

"Unbelievable." Charley slammed the heel of his hand against his forehead and rolled his eyes toward the flawless blue sky.

"They say they can be charged with energy, so I was just wondering if when I was standing on that vortex with my crystal if, you know, it could have made the vortex's energy increase."

"That vortex isn't a radio, and besides, that's not even what crystals do for radios."

"What do you mean a vortex isn't a radio?"

"Well, you said that they say crystals have energy and that you thought maybe they could increase the energy of a vortex. It just made me think of crystal transistors. But crystals don't have any energy at all in themselves."

"This'll be a big blow to Andrea and others."

"Well, they don't. If an energy source is applied, as in radios, through electrical current, they can amplify and switch electrical signals. That's the whole basis of solid-state radios. But even then it has to be a certain kind of crystal. Doped crystals, they call them."

"But they don't cure anxiety and back pain?"

"No . . . at least not that I've ever heard of. I think that Bell laboratories could have figured that out if they figured out solid state radios."

"Loy McClure thinks they helped her with her disk problem."

"Who's Loy McClure?"

"One of the counselors at the ranch."

"Amy, I can't believe the crap they're feeding you guys. I mean, aren't there any adults there with functioning brains? You don't have to be a Ph.D in physics to know this a load of crap. How can they swallow this . . . this mumbo jumbo?"

Amy shrugged, but her brow puckered.

# 12 _____ Amy had Brian drop her off at the gate of Rancho Radiance. He would have needed a special pass now to get in, so it was just easier for her to walk the mile to the main compound. She spotted the first tent less than a quarter mile past the main gate into Rancho Radiance. Domes of shimmering colors billowed from the red, rubbly land like enormous prickly pear cactus. These were the rainbow-hued dome tents that could be bought through Rancho Radiance's mail-order catalogue. Carefully constructed to maximize the pos-

itive energies of the vortex region, each tent came with its own double-terminated quartz crystal in a pocket sewn into a seam at the apex of the dome. The two-person tents sold for three hundred dollars each. The four-to-six person one sold for four hundred and seventy-five. Amy realized that these tents were now popping up across the landscape thicker than flies.

The faithful had begun to arrive the day before for the summer solstice celebration. It would take place over two weekends and was bigger than Christmas for the Pahatties. Tomorrow Pahata Ra herself would arrive after an exhausting three-week trip to England and France, where she had held over one hundred public and private audiences in which she channeled the ancient spirit of Lamata Ra, the sovereign entity, her teacher and cosmic guide, whose knowledge she shared with the world. The fees ranged from one hundred to four hundred dollars for an audience; private ones came considerably higher.

Amy noticed that tucked discreetly behind stands of Arizona sycamores were banks of rainbow-painted port-a-potties. Between the gate and the main ranch house at least ten food vendors had opened stands that served everything from fruit kebabs to falafel sandwiches. She sighed as she remembered the nice steak sandwiches she and Charley had packed for lunch, leftovers from the archaeology camp's dinner the night before.

As she drew closer to the main compound she tried to focus her mind and think harder about precisely how she would go about this business. She had to play her cards right. This was important to her. Charley was about the cutest guy she'd ever seen—but it wasn't just that he was awesomely cute. He was smart, he was normal, and she really liked his mom and Archie. Now, for the first time in her life, she could do something to help someone accomplish something important.

She had never been called upon to do anything in her life except behave herself and go along as her mom moved through husbands and lifestyles. She was either good—sickeningly good, like when her mom was with a neat man that she liked or in a situation that she enjoyed—or sullen, as now, when she was at

Rancho Radiance and it looked as if David Many Hearts was becoming the next man in Barbara Stanton's life. Amy shuddered when she thought about her mom and David.

Of course Ralph was still around. Amy had liked Ralph all right. He was innocuous, a wimp really, but on occasion he had stood up for Amy and he was certainly trying to put the best face on things as he watched his marriage disintegrate out here in the desert. Amy almost had the feeling that Ralph was staying around as much for her sake as for his own. But she didn't know how much help he would be in this business. "Business," she realized, was not the right word. Business was selling rainbow tents with sewn-in crystals to thousands. This was a mission, and she had embarked on it on behalf of Archie Baldwin. He needed to dig that site. There was no logical reason why he shouldn't—only mumbo jumbo. But of course she couldn't say that—that was where playing her cards right became crucial. You just couldn't come right out and say, Look, this is all a bunch of crap. There's no special power here or around here that is going to be disturbed by Archie Baldwin digging.

She was wondering just how much she could confide in Ralph—not that he would tell, but how stable was he these days? God, she was sick of having to be the adult in this family! She spotted him as she approached the compound now. He was walking from the facilitation center where all the therapy groups met. On this bright day he seemed engulfed in his own shadow, his shoulders hunched forward, his head bent, his chin tucked in, his hands jammed deep in his pockets. He appeared to be imploding. He was beyond therapy, that was for sure.

No, she couldn't enlist him in her mission. He was too caught up in his own problems, like everyone else here. That, of course, had been the great relief in meeting up with Charley, Amy thought suddenly. You could stop thinking about yourself or Pahata Ra. Charley had shown her what he was doing with computers. Through him she met the whole archaeological team and then his mom. They thought about other things—rocks, Indians who had lived here thousands of years ago, computers, children's books. It was all so much more interesting. It was actually the children's books that Amy was counting on to pave the way with her mom, at least getting her interested in Archie's case. Her mom would have kittens when she found out that Charley's mom was none other than Calista Jacobs, the famous book illustrator. Charley had never mentioned this until his mom got there, and at first Amy herself didn't know the name—just the books. *Sky Boy* and *Nick in the Night* had been her all-time favorite bedtime stories from the time she was about four until she was seven or eight, and her mother had loved them too. So it was just possible that her mother would be so impressed that she would go to Pahata herself with the request. After all, Barbara Stanton had spent a lifetime basking in the reflected light of people she considered creative, and she already did like Charley a bunch, felt he had a wonderful influence on Amy, influence here meaning removal of a sullen child from her mother's presence.

"Hi, Amy! Want to help put up some of these balloons for the welcome?"

"Sure." Amy walked over to where a young woman stood tethering balloons. She wore her hair in four long braids that descended from under a bandanna tied pirate style.

"I'm so excited," the young woman said. Her name was Shinon. It had been magnetically derived two summers before from the same vortex as Amy's so they were considered "monadic sisters," or "sisters in resonance," which meant that they were supposed to have a lot in common. Amy did not feel this was so at all, but she still did like Shinon.

"What about?" Amy said.

"What about?" The girl stepped back and looked with disbelief at Amy. "Rainbow Da!" Amy rolled her eyes. She just hated it when people called her that. "Don't you realize what's happening tomorrow, who's coming?"

"Oh yeah."

"My goodness, you could show a little more enthusiasm, Da."

"Shinon, when you were my age would this have turned you on?"

"When I was your age I was a vegetable. I was spending my days sitting around at a country club in Rye, New York, worrying about my next pair of designer jeans. You don't know how lucky you are to have such an enlightened mother to bring you here. I had to find my way on my own. I had to go through drugs. My parents had me committed to fancy mental hospitals. I had electric shock therapy. Count your blessings."

Amy sighed and took a balloon. There was no sense even trying to talk to someone like Shinon. She stayed around for a few minutes and helped string up several more balloons, then headed toward the small cabin that she and her mom and Ralph occupied. On the way she passed the Guardians of the Petal Way. These were woman specially chosen to weave the floral carpet runner on which Pahata always walked when she descended from her helicopter on returning home. Smaller carpets of mums were woven and placed at her feet when she channeled the spirit of Lamata. It was a great honor to be a floral weaver. The mums were a particularly hardy variety that were resistant to heat as well as to being stepped upon. They were flown in from a farm that Pahata owned in Washington State that specialized in growing the flowers that were sold by the faithful in airports and bus terminals. As the women wove they chanted a mantra that only they were allowed to use. When sections of the carpet were completed they were stored in a walk-in refrigerator in the main commissary.

To the right of where the Guardians of the Petal Way were weaving their flowers, a tent with open sides had been erected over a raised wooden platform. Here twenty male and female dancers were moving to the rhythmic beat of two bongo drums as they practiced the Spiral Dance. Loy McClure stood in front of the group leading them. Amy paused a moment to watch. Loy was the best of the dancers. She had a fantastic figure that she did not do much to conceal. Amy could see her breasts moving under the diaphanous tie-dyed tunic she wore. Her arms and hands were particularly graceful and expressive. She signaled the drummers to stop.

"Okay now, folks. I am seeing too much of this." She held her arms straight out stiffly. "Remember, we are talking about a cosmic form here. The symmetry comes from the motion itself and motion cannot become symmetrical if it is stiff. You need to bend those arms slightly, curve them, and do a half rotation of each arm. This is how you are going to achieve a more perfect balance ultimately. This is the balance of the galaxy. This is the source of the spiral movement, and like the developing stages of galaxies, we extend our center of energy and light out into the universe through these spiraling motions. It's basically the same idea of what I talk about in my gonadic-vibrations class—we want to achieve orgasm not through taking but by giving way and opening those chakras that in turn lead to the opening of inter-dimensional doorways that allow for that powerful alliance. . . ." Loy waved merrily at Amy as she caught her eye.

Amy like Loy a lot. She was not quite sure what Loy's therapy really involved. It was one of the few therapy classes that her mother did not make her go to. Loy had apparently been an actress of some sort before she had met up with Pahata Ra and found her way to the Rainbow Bridge of Enlightenment. But Loy was always cheerful and upbeat. Not that people at Rancho Radiance tended to be sad. That was hardly the case, but they were inclined toward being blissful rather than cheerful. In states of sheer bliss they just beamed and rarely said much except to tell you how blissed out they were. Loy was genuinely cheerful in a kind of good, old-fashioned, bubbly way. She bounced along when she walked, cracked jokes (nobody ever cracked jokes around the ranch), and when she laughed it was a nice, deep chortle.

Amy cut through the classroom building. There was only one class going on there now. She could hear the unmistakable voice. A queasiness began in her stomach. "And so we can see through a clear demonstration the reality of these vibrational frequencies as they exist in the auric field through the use of Radionic antennae. It is a deceptively simple device."

David Many Hearts was giving a lecture on the reality of the human aura and how it could be measured. Amy wondered how his device would stack up against Charley's Time Slicer. She hurried by, daring only to give the quickest glance into the classroom. There appeared to be only about five or six people in the class, and she was surprised not to see her mother. The building seemed empty, but as she passed another door slightly ajar she saw Andrea applying a crystal to someone reclining on a couch.

She exited the classroom building through a back door. Her mother and stepfather's cabin was just twenty yards away. She thought she heard a loud voice as she approached. She slowed her step immediately and quietly walked up the steps of the porch.

"I'm very sorry, Barbara, but I just cannot accept that as a rational solution to our problems."

"This is not our problem, Ralph. It is *your* problem," Amy heard her mother hiss. "I have availed myself of every therapy that I thought would help this marriage. Three months ago I was very nearly frigid."

Oh shit, thought Amy. She was so sick of hearing about her mother's orgasms or lack of them. "I want you to see Loy," Barbara said in a low, steady voice. "It is our only chance."

"Barbara, I don't know what you're talking about. I really don't think that we solve these problems by . . . by . . . promiscuous behavior."

"Goddammit, Ralph, I can't believe you! You are so hemmed in, you are so anal." Oh, great, now her mother was calling Ralph anal. Well, better that her mother focus on Ralph than on herself, Amy thought. "You think it's dirty, don't you? It is not promiscuous. It is therapy. Masters and Johnson's masterwork was based on precisely this kind of thing—sexual surrogates."

"Well, then I'd rather go to Masters and Johnson than a former porn star."

"Loy was not a porn star!"

Loy was a porn star! Jeez Louise! There was a long silence.

Maybe this was the time she could make her entrance. She had work to do, after all. She crept back down the stairs then ran up again noisily as if she were just arriving and hadn't heard a word.

"Hi, guys! I'm back," Amy said, bursting into the room.

"Oh, Da Da, you look so happy and wonderful. Did you have fun with Charley? He's such a nice boy."

"He is great, Mom, and guess what? You will just never believe it in a million years. Guess who his mom is?"

**13**————————— "I just can't believe it." Barbara Stanton shook her head in wonder. "I think that is so exciting, Da. She must be a lovely woman. And you say this Archie Baldwin fellow is her boyfriend?"

Amy nodded. "And all he really wants to do, Mom, is dig this site that's on a corner of the ranch. Swami Ben-Ji Prem La is dead set against it, but the people in these parts have always let Archie dig. He's really a big shot in the field. As a matter of fact, Charley said that he was once the head of the department of archaeology at the Smithsonian, but he quit because it was too much administration stuff. And he teaches at Harvard, too, along with his work at the Smithsonian." She paused a moment to let that sink in. She knew her mother well and had perfected her timing. She opened her eyes a little wider and leaned slightly forward. "He even wrote the book, Mom."

"What book?" Barbara asked.

"The book on American archaeology, the one they use in all the college courses."

"Oh my God!" Barbara slapped her cheek softly as the light began to dawn. "His name's Archibald Baldwin isn't it?"

"Yes."

"Oh my God!" she said again. "I think I remember that text, from my freshman archaeology course at Bennington!"

"They had textbooks at Bennington?" Ralph said with as much of an edge as his voice could ever hone.

But Barbara was in such rapture that she ignored the comment. "Ralph, this guy is famous!"

Amy had played her cards right. Her mother was a sucker for authorities—in any field from the divine to archaeology, from children's books to therapy, from astrology to rolfing, she sought out the best. That her child, her dear, recalcitrant, sullen, exasperating Amy had made friends with these extraordinary people was proof for Barbara Stanton that the charts were right, her beliefs vindicated, and her own parents were absolutely wrong in criticizing her for her methods of child rearing. She felt not just vindicated but positively ebullient. What a rich life she had indeed given her daughter on both the divine and the secular level. And to think that Amy had wanted to go on one of those teen tours of America where rich kids took Greyhound buses to Las Vegas and Disneyland. Her grandparents had even offered to pay for it. But Barbara had provided the ultimate mind-expanding experience. Here her daughter and only child had come into the presence of the divine and ancient soul of Lamata Ra as manifested through Pahata Ra as well as the best the secular world had to offer—a master children's book illustrator and the man who had written *the* textbook on North American archaeology, not to mention the child prodigy Charley, who Ralph himself said was a genius! It was too good to be true. She couldn't wait to call her parents and tell them how wonderfully this summer, for which they had predicted disaster, was turning out.

Of course she would do her best with Pahata Ra on behalf of Archie. It seemed to be the one thing that both she and Ralph agreed upon—that there could be no real harm done. And as Ralph had pointed out, if all the other ranchers and people in the region had allowed Archie to dig over the last twenty years, it certainly would not look good if Rancho Radiance was the only holdout. Barbara was simply dying to meet Archie and Calista. She would tell them herself that she would act on Archie's behalf and go directly to Pahata Ra. So she and Ralph and Amy decided to drive over immediately.

The sooner the better, Amy thought. She wanted to set things in action immediately, before David Many Hearts got wind of it. In Amy's mind David Many Hearts was much more of a problem than Swami Ben-ji by virtue of the fact that he exercised a lot more influence on her mom than Ben-ji did.

If Pahata said no, that was one thing. But if Barbara never even got a chance to go to Pahata just because David discouraged her, or said no, well, that was something else. The success of this plan depended on Barbara's having clear access to Pahata. And she usually did have that access, because God knew, or rather Pahata knew, how much money Barbara had poured into this operation. She had turned over great chunks of IBM and Lilly stock to Pahata's foundation. It was part of the settlement from her second husband. She couldn't touch any of Amy's portfolio or her own trust fund. Amy's grandfather had made sure of that.

Calista saw the Mercedes station wagon driving up to camp and wondered who it could be. Then Amy popped out. My God, Calista thought slowly, she must have done it. Charley had said she was going to try to get her mom to intervene. Now Calista was trying to reconcile the image of the woman walking toward her with the notion of someone who had dropped all to follow someone she had believed was God into the desert. Barbara Stanton wore a new cowboy hat, a white woven one, the kind designed for summer wear on the range that allowed for cool ventilating breezes. Her dark hair was carefully arranged under her hat. Her eyeshadow matched the large chunky amethyst earrings, and descending into her deep cleavage were a few more slivers of amethyst. That must be her signature crystal—cured everything except the trouble those brand-new boots were still giving. She walked toward Calista smiling broadly and extending her hand, but her feet really hurt her, and the pain made her walk as if she were pinching a penny between her buttocks.

"I am so pleeezed to meet you. I recognize you from your book jackets." The words came in a long, sweet ooze. She was definitely more Beverly Hills than Scarsdale, but it was darn nice of her to say that Calista still looked like her book jackets because the books she must have been reading when Amy was a little kid had to be ten years old. Behind her walked a very nondescript man. That must be Ralph, Calista thought. Charley had described him as a dead ringer for Mister Rogers. Fairly accurate. And according to Charley, Rancho Radiance was not his neighborhood and their marriage was about to crack. He looked very pleased to be here, though, and came forward and began pumping her hand vigorously.

"Ralph . . . Ralph Stanton. We're so pleased to meet you. Charley's made such a difference for Amy."

There was a lot of small talk. Calista caught Barbara Stanton looking over her shoulder at something. She turned around. Oh God! What an entrance! Archie was just coming from the outhouse and was still zipping his fly. She should put up a sign: Men kindly arrange clothing before leaving the premises.

"Oh!" Barbara expostulated. "That must be Archibald Baldwin." He'd just finished zipping his fly. "You know, I had his textbook in my freshman archaeology course at Bennington. I must tell him." She began to totter toward him in her boots, which Calista could actually hear creak. Oh, Archie was just going to love this! She watched him sort out what was happening. First the perplexed look as Barbara Stanton came wobbling toward him, then the flicker of recognition, the slight smile. Now did that smile coincide with the moment when Calista thought she saw his eyes lower toward the prepossessing bosom with its crystal-studded cleavage?

Calista began to flutter about in the semblance of the perfect desert hostess. "Would you like the house special?" They were sitting around an empty lab tent table. Steve had set out some chips and guacomole.

"What's that?" Barbara said.

"A petrone—vodka and Gatorade. It's not as bad as it sounds."

"Oh, we don't drink alcohol," Barbara quickly answered.

"Well, now Barb . . ." Ralph began to say.

"Oh, Ralph, you just can't. It really does mess up the crystal therapy and you have a session tomorrow." Archie and Calista both nodded politely. "Ralph has had this terrible problem with a vertebra in his neck, oh, for years now. It became particularly bad in recent months, but you know, since he's begun his crystal therapy with Andrea he has not had to wear his neck brace once."

"Well, I'm not sure if it's that or just the climate. You know this hot dry climate is wonderful for that kind of thing." While Ralph spoke, he longingly eyed the vodka bottle Archie had extracted from the bottom drawer of a filing cabinet that served as a bar.

"No, no." Barbara swung her head emphatically. "Do you know what a hematite stone is?" She looked directly at Calista.

"Well, I've heard of it. I guess maybe I've seen one. They're very dark, aren't they?"

"Yes, almost black. Well, Andrea has Ralph sleep with one in a little bag that ties underneath his chin, but you see the bag with the stone is on top of his head." Barbara pointed to the crown of her own head with a long manicured nail.

Calista had started to bite her lip. Oh God, she knew she was going to laugh. "Yes," she said, and got up to walk to the cooler nearby, from which she removed a bottle of fruit juice.

"Oh, that'll be fine," Barbara said, seeing the bottle of juice. "Because, see, alcohol really screws it all up. So Ralph has been sleeping with this hematite stone right on top of his head, right at the crown, and then at the center of his back, just above the tailbone he tapes a small amethyst." She pointed to her amethyst earrings—not the ones sliding down her boobs. "Andrea experimented with several crystal layout plans and this seems to be the one that is really working. You see, the idea is to open all the chakras. . . ."

Calista dared not look at Archie, not even a glance. They

would both crack up if their eyes met even for a millisecond. But the notion of this man, who looked indeed just like Mister Rogers, with all of these stones strapped to him was too much. She felt a laugh coming up. Oh no! This was worse than labor pains. God, the mere picture of Ralph with his little bag tied to his head. She began to cough wildly to camouflage the laugh. Archie jumped up. "I'm fine . . . fine." But tears were squeezing out of her eyes. Just excuse me a second."

She ran to the outhouse. With her luck, they would think she was choking to death, follow her, and try to revive her with the Heimlich maneuver. Was there such a thing as terminal laughter?

She had to compose herself. What if she were responsible for blowing Archie's only hopes for digging Los Gatos! She sat down on the toilet seat and tried to have sober thoughts. She stared hard. The outhouse's primary decorating scheme was people's diplomas from various institutions. Archie's were there too—his B.A. from Dartmouth, his Ph.D from Harvard, along with a few honorary degrees. Also included was a little certificate from a Mrs. Grey's school of ballroom dancing, the most proper of all the Boston dancing schools, of which Archie was a 1945 graduate and thereby declared fit material for the waltz evenings when he had steered various Warren and Saltonstall cousins around the floor to the music of Ruby Newman.

This, he had reported, had done very little to quell his raging hormones. Calista now tried to imagine Archie dancing and the sheer torture of those evenings he had described. She tried to imagine him studying at Dartmouth, at Harvard, writing his books, figuring out the projectile-point typology for which he had gained his reputation. She tried the most serious and proper thoughts imaginable, but nothing could eradicate the image of Ralph Stanton with a little stone tied to his head. She began laughing so hard that she doubled over on the toilet seat and tears rolled down her cheeks.

Finally, however, she did compose herself, and when she returned to the group they were mercifully off the topic of crystals and Ralph's vertebra problem. Archie was listening attentively as

Barbara spoke about intervening on his behalf with Pahata Ra.

"I wish you could both come tomorrow when she arrives. It's going to be a glorious festival," she said, turning to Calista.

"I can't," Archie was saying. "But maybe Calista and Charley would like to go."

"Oh, would you?"Amy sprang up.

"Her arrivals are really something!" Ralph said.

"They air-drop rose petals by the ton!" Amy exclaimed. "And there are acrobats."

"It's a wonderful festival. Do come, Calista."

"Oh no. I really . . . er . . . uh. It sounds wonderful and all that, but I really wanted to go over to this other site with Archie and see what he's been up to. However, Charley, why don't you go?"

It was decided that Charley would return with Amy and her mother and Ralph.


Calista was already in the sleeping bag and reading by a battery lamp suspended from the top of the tent when Archie came in. His face looked troubled. "They're calling off the search for Tonk?" she said. He started unbuttoning his shirt. "It just doesn't make sense. The guy has vanished without a trace." He paused. "I mean without a trace and . . ." He stopped again.

"And what?" Calista pushed up her reading glasses into the thick mass of silvery chestnut hair piled on her head.

"And Claudie. That doesn't make sense either."

"Do you think the two are related some way?"

"I'm not sure. Agnes Bessie is trying to figure out who Claudie would have been visiting over in Yuma." He pulled off his boots and then his pants. It was cold. The temperature drops were dramatic after the sun went down.

Against one side of the tent there was a plastic box with small drawers, the kind that might be used for keeping bolts or washers in, small objects. Archie used it for interesting fragments that he found each day at the site, ones that he did not immediately take to the lab tent but wanted to look at a little longer, study a bit more. He crawled over to it now on his hands and knees, muttering about Claudie and Tonk. He was clearly disturbed, and when he was disturbed he liked to sort through these small treasures. It was as much of a meditative exercise as anything else. He didn't have to be in the field to do it. Calista had seen him do the same thing elsewhere. He was like a child in this sense. He carried his precious things around with him.

When he visited her house in Cambridge, in his briefcase he would often have a small pouch of carefully wrapped pieces—fragments of pottery, projectile points, bone, whatever. This was the archaeologist's currency, after all. He would pull them out and simply think. She did not know what he was thinking exactly, whether he was actually contemplating the ancient world of the prehistoric hunter or the first artisan who had crafted these pieces. There was always the faint scent of sagebrush—or was it juniper?—when he opened these drawers or pouches. Calista wasn't sure which, but it was definitely Archie's scent. It was as if that high desert country still clung to him, whether he was in Cambridge or Washington.

The dual appointment at Harvard and the Smithsonian had come through rather conveniently, just as their affair was commencing. But Calista now thought she could in all honesty call it a relationship and not just an affair. He spent one semester, the fall semester, in Cambridge. The spring one he was in Washington but commuted one day a week to Cambridge for a graduate seminar he taught. It was nice. He had fitted nicely into their family. He had been reluctant to take over Tom's study as his own. Said he didn't need one. But Calista had insisted, "It doesn't bother me. It wouldn't bother Tom. Tom contemplated the universe and its origins. You're just doing the closer-range picture—earth and its people. It's all part of the same continuum. I'm not into shrines for knowledge. I'm into continuous knowing. So there."

So there. There was no arguing with that sort of bedrock common sense. He had moved his stuff into the study. He liked the spectacular astronomy photographs—the ones of the weird starry configurations like the Crab Nebula, Cygnus X, solar-wind shots from various space flights, or the Jet Propulsion Lab at Cal Tech. The picture of Richard Feynman Charley had claimed and taken up to his bedroom. But Archie had added a few of his own. It was a comfortable arrangement all the way around. Calista looked at him now, bent over contemplating his booty. God, it was so cold! How could he stand it?

"Archie, you make me cold just to look at you."

"Hmmm." He was lost in thought.

"You've got goose bumps and other bumps are receding." She giggled.

"Cold enough, in other words, to turn a man into a boy?" He looked up at her now. And smiled. His eyes twinkling behind the half glasses that had slipped down his nose. "You could get a rise out of that one."

She laughed again. He put the pieces back into the little drawers and scrambled over to the sleeping bag.

"God, your buns are freezing!" she gasped as he tucked in beside her. She pulled him close to her. "Here turn over, put them right there." She snuggled her stomach up to his backside.

"Put your hands right there," he said and grabbed her hand that was around his chest and guided it downward.

"Wait, let me take off my glasses," she said, reaching up into the morass of her hair.

"They don't need glasses."

"You're really a card!"

"What are you reading?"

"Jane Austen—*Persuasion*. Speaking of which."

"Yes."

"I was wondering what Jane Austen would make of Barbara and Ralph Stanton."

"You were, were you?"

"Yes, I was wondering if she would find them 'clever'."

"Clever?"

"Yes, or really good company. I just finished reading one of those wonderful pure Austen passages. You know, where she does one of her numbers on manners or people's behavior."

"Yeah, and you want to know what she'd make of Barbara and Ralph and the crystal tied to his head."

Calista giggled again. "Well, she said—Jane, that is, that her notion of good company was that of 'clever, well-informed people who have a great deal to say,' and given that definition I was just wondering if Barbara and Ralph with all their crystal talk might measure up."

"Do I have to answer while you're doing to me what you are doing to me?" Calista laughed deep in her throat and licked his shoulder blade. "Because I do think I'm measuring up."

"Admirably."

**14**————————"We are talking here about higher force fields in which motion is dependent upon order, or what we call here the Merkabean template."

Charley was trying to follow this as best he could. There were smatterings of concepts that he knew about, but somehow they trailed off into vacuums of misstated references and butchered physics. Mostly, however, it was wrong words, grafted onto bastardized notions, just as now, when David Many Hearts was giving a lecture to a packed room on biosatellites, also known as Merkabahs. In one swift phrase he was destroying the whole notion of quantum mechanics and the uncertainty principle: "You see," he was saying, his hands gesticulating and his long hair flying as he strode across the room in front of a blackboard, "the Merkabean template is merely a grid for atoms that are traveling on a particular frequency of light."

Charley leaned over and cupped his hands around Amy's ear. "Photons, not atoms, travel in light waves or frequencies." Forget the fact that quantum mechanics said that there was no grid, no order or predictable course for these particles, was this man really suggesting that atoms traveled at light speed? Charley could not imagine what he was proposing.

Amy turned toward him and cupped her hands over his ear now. Charley felt a little thrill and something prickle on the back of his neck as her warm breath hit his ear. "You mean, can't travel at all?"

No! No! No! he thought, but it was not a denial of her question. Oh God, he was glad he was sitting down and nobody could see what was happening in his pants. He scrunched around and tried to cross his legs and then leaned forward. A little physics ought to put a damper on things. He cupped his hands again over her ears. Her ears smelled good, not like earwax. He bet his smelled like earwax. He'd have to remember to ask his mom for some Q-Tips. "Atoms can travel, sure, but if they travel at light speed . . ." And, indeed, David Many Hearts was just that moment saying that they did. Charley paused and then resumed, "Anything with any mass at all when traveling at light speed would acquire infinite mass. It's not possible for matter to travel at light speed—not even Merkabahs."

David Many Hearts was continuing. "It is through Merkabahs, then, that human evolution will be transported into the blue-white star fields of Population 2 Life systems. Prior to this, of course, is a preparatory phase in order that mankind can handle the great energies that emanate from these biosatellites." Not to mention, Charley thought, the lack of oxygen, and heavy-duty radiation once you get there. And what the hell was a blue-white star field or Population 2 Life systems? Again David Many Hearts but Few Brains was making an incomprehensible hash of things.

There were blue horizontal branch stars that in fact were called Population 2 stars. They were the older stars as opposed to Population 1 stars such as the sun. But blue-white? White dwarfs were those shrunken hot white stars of high surface temperature and low density. Now what was this guy talking about? Not a place you'd want to go to even in a Merkabah or evolve to or whatever. It was becoming more and more unbelievable.

"Part of the preparation for entering the blue-white star field is developing a sufficient consciousness. When this does happen and one can subsequently understand the true evolutionary purpose of the Merkabah, you are then in tune with the grid and the portal of the vehicle is opened up to you. This is no simple hatch. This is an energy portal which emits a blue-white light in quanta measured to your own vibrational rates and creates an energy field around the body to protect it as the body is taken into the vehicle and makes the ascent up the staircase of crystal energy. I thank you."

There was a burst of applause as David Many Hearts dipped his head down in a terse but humble nod that was part of a bow signifying the end of his session.

"Unbelievable!" Charley muttered.

"Isn't it?" A middle-aged woman sitting in front of them turned around. "I came here all the way from Sacramento. It's the second time I've heard him speak. He's sensational, isn't he?" She was in such a blissful state herself that she failed to see that Charley and Amy didn't nod in agreement, although Charley did try to smile politely.

"I think it's just wonderful to see youngsters like you so interested in all of this. You know, it's really about continuing evolution. I hope you're planning on going to the preparatory sessions. They're a little expensive, but I think if you're really planning to apply for that first flight in 2,002, it's advisable. You're young; you should do it." She patted Amy on the knee. This almost made Charley puke. *We're young, we should do it! We should get on a space ship and evolve. I just want to grow up; forget evolving. I'm not even a sexually active adolescent homo sapiens yet. Oh, bug off, lady!*

"So you think David Many Hearts is full of crap?" Amy asked as they left the building.

"Think? I know."

"Well, my mom's having an affair with him."

"You mean she's sleeping with him?"

"Yep."

"Do you know for sure?"

"Yep, and don't ask how. It was really embarrassing."

"You mean you walked in on them or something?" He blushed furiously. "Oh, I'm sorry. I didn't mean to ask."

"Don't be sorry." Amy kicked a rock with the toe of her shoe. "But, yes. It was kind of embarrassing. It's not the first time she's had affairs while she's been married to somebody, just the first time I . . . er . . . saw it happening."

"Well, what did she say to you?"

" 'Get out!' " Amy laughed.

"I mean after that?"

"Oh, she was really nice to me. Didn't want me to tell Ralph, I guess, not that I would have. But basically she tried to pass it off as part of her therapy, continuing evolution, you know."

"You mean to get into the Merkabah you have to have sex with David before you can go to the blue white-star fields. Gee Han Solo didn't do that."

"Who's Han Solo?"

"Remember *Star Wars* and the Millennium Falcon? It traveled at lightspeed. Him and Chewbacca."

Amy laughed. "Oh yeah. Well, I don't think it was a specific part of that Merkabah preparation course he was talking about, just part of the general stuff he's been working on with Mom."

"Oh, God, Amy, I don't envy you. I mean your mom seems so basically nice. How can she go for this guy? He's such a turkey."

Amy squeezed her eyes shut tight, trying to erase the image she had seen when she had walked into the room of her mother and David Many Hearts together, a naked tangle of sweaty loins, flashes of pubic hair, and moans. She had fled, run straight outside, and thrown up in some bushes.

And as if that weren't bad enough, it had only gotten worse

when her mother had tried to explain. Amy hadn't wanted to talk about it at all. She wouldn't have told Ralph. She had no desire to make any trouble. She had just wanted to fade away, become a ghost within her own family. But no. It couldn't be. Her mother kept bringing it up, trying to justify it, and now there had been a new twist. Her mother said that David said that the three of them needed to sit down and discuss the true meaning of this experience.

At first Amy had thought that they meant David, Ralph, and her mother. Fine. It was their problem—let them do it. But no. David hadn't meant that at all. They wanted to discuss it with her! She had said straight out that it was the worst idea she had ever heard of. There was no way she would ever sit down and discuss this with them. It was their problem, not hers. But David was so slippery. He always turned around what you were saying. It was her problem. She had to face her sexuality and blah, blah, blah. They wouldn't let it go. The pressure had been mounting. She was scared. She didn't know what to do and the last thing she would ever do was tell Charley Jacobs about it. But here she'd already let it slip about walking in on her mom and David. God, sometimes she felt so lonely. Tears had started to stream down Amy's face now.

"Amy, what's wrong? You're crying."

"Oh, it's nothing." But a sob swelled up within her and burst. She curled her hands into fists and pressed them into her face. Her shoulders hunched over. Small tremors wracked her body. Charley was flabbergasted. He stood back, stunned. He didn't know what to do. He was neary transfixed. There was something about the way her narrow shoulders shook under the spread of her thick, curly hair that touched something at his very center. He put his arm around her. "Let's get out of here."

He led her off to a secluded area beyond the compound where no tents had been pitched and there was no one about. She felt like a knot, a tight wet knot under his arm. "It's going to be okay, Amy. It's going to be okay."

He didn't know how it was going to be okay and it really just made him feel better to say it than it probably made her, he thought. But the more he said it the stronger he seemed to feel. Maybe just somebody there saying it was going to be okay, someone who really cared about her might make a little difference, might be the first little step toward okayness for Amy. But he wasn't sure what that meant.

They had sat down on a large rock that marked the beginning of a hiking trail down into one of the small canyons that gouged the ranch property. Amy seemed composed now. She sniffled noisily and wiped her eyes.

"Look, Charley . . . this is like really kind of painful for me and I just can't talk about it. So please don't ask me too much."

"I won't, but . . ."

"Don't worry, Charley. I can handle this. My mom's a complete flake. I've been through a lot with her. I can take this."

Charley was perplexed. What did she mean she could handle this? This was all wrong. She wasn't supposed to handle this. Parents were supposed to handle this kind of stuff. His mother handled everything. Charley didn't get his mother through things. It was the reverse. She did it for him. Amy saw the frankly bewildered look in Charley's eyes.

"If it gets too bad I just go to my grandparents. But don't worry. I kind of lost it back there, that's all. David Many Hearts is a real creep."


Pahata Ra would be arriving within the hour. And the tension was mounting. They could detect it as they neared the compound. They had just passed the helicopter landing pad where the Guardians of the Petal Way were watering the carpet of flowers in preparation when David Many Hearts turned from the clump of people he was with and walked toward Amy and Charley.

"Rainbow Da! And Charley. How you doin', guys? I see you were at my Merkabah lecture. How did you like it?"

Oh, Jeez, thought Charley. This was going to be hard. "It was interesting."

"Oh yeah? What did you find interesting?" His voice sounded

languid but when he slid up his mirrored sunglasses into his long straight black hair his pale amber eyes seemed brittle. This guy's after me, Charley thought. He knew it as certainly as he had ever known anything. He felt his heart beat a little faster. He had to move very carefully here.

"Oh, I don't know." He kicked lightly at the dirt with the toe of his shoe. "You know, it's just interesting and all that."

"No questions?"

"Well, I was a little confused about the blue-white star field and the Population 2 life systems."

"What confused you?"

"I just never heard Population 2 used in reference to life systems before." He refrained from elaborating that his father had written a paper once on Pop 2 stars, which were older stars with relatively low abundances of metals that were found in globular clusters or the nuclear bulge of a galaxy.

"Oh, really these Population 2 life systems are extensions, or perhaps we should say, distillations, of the harmonic energy of the universe."

This did not clear things up for Charley, and he was not particularly adept in terms of camouflaging his confusion. "Oh," he said rather unconvincingly.

David Many Hearts sighed as if he were dealing with some sort of New Age dyslexic. "Tell me, Charley."

"Yeah?"

"Do you believe that the harmonic energy of the world is loving?"

"Huh?"

"Do you believe that these universal magnetic vibrations that produce cosmic harmonies of the universe are loving?"

This was an unanswerable question as far as Charley was concerned. "I . . . I . . ." he stammered, "I just don't know. I guess I never thought of energy or the universe as being described as having love or hate."

"Well, what word would you use to describe the universe?" David Many Hearts persisted.

"Maybe order—a kind of mathematical order."

"Just maybe?"

"Yeah, I mean, who's to know? That's what particle physicists are working on, that's why they're building these humongous atom smashers."

"But how would we define this order in relation to ourselves?"

"I never thought of it that way—in relation to ourselves."

"But if there is order that must mean that there is a plan for all living things."

"Maybe."

"Maybe?" David shook his head in a gesture of dramatic disbelief.

"But there might not be any order," Charley said.

"You mean no mathematical equation."

"Yeah, and even if there is, it might not relate to us. Maybe the universe doesn't care about us? I don't know." Charley had grown up around scientists, and many physicists. He was simply not used to having conversations take this form. He was accustomed to hearing people, many of them including his father distinguished intellects, couch their speculations in conditional terms—words like "maybe" and "if," "possibly" and "perhaps." These words were the coin of the theoretical physicist's realm, of men and women who sought to probe the meaning of the universe and possibly God's mind through the available tools of relativity, quantum mechanics, notions and equations pertaining to the Big Bang, black holes, and the Doppler Effect. But David Many Hearts never said "maybe" except in mockery, for he had all the answers and was addicted to the terms of the absolute.

"Oh, come on, Charley, I think you know more than you're letting on. I hear your father is a big gun Harvard astrophysicist."

Charley looked up straight into the amber eyes. "You're wrong."

"I'm wrong?" David Many Hearts was caught off guard.

"My father is dead," Charley said.

· · ·

At that moment a pneumatic beating seized the air and out of the impeccably blue skies a dark little spider jittered.

"Ah-yeee!" The sound rolled across the ranch as nearly a thousand people stopped whatever they were doing and began to chant.

"What's happening?" Charley whispered to Amy.

"She's coming."

"But what are they all moaning about—or is that a mantra?"

"Not technically. It's Pahata's deep-degree resonator. Kind of like her basic chord."

"Was it magnetically derived, like yours?" Charley asked.

"Not exactly, but I don't quite understand the difference."

"What don't you understand, dear?" At that moment Barbara Stanton came up behind them and put her arms around both Amy and Charley. She gave them an affectionate squeeze. "Isn't this exciting, children? She's coming home!"

"I was just explaining about the Ah-yeee, Mom. I don't understand about how deep-degree resonators differ from, you know, magnetically derived ones like my name."

"Now see, Amy, if you had attended that joint lecture that Andrea and Swami Ben-ji gave, you would have been able to explain it. The deep-degree resonators are the ones that were derived from the minerals of Atlantis."

"Atlantis?" Charley asked.

"The lost continent where the original souls, the divine . . ." She stopped speaking and began chanting the Ah-yeee. The helicopter was now on its final approach, and thousands of rose petals had been jettisoned from a hatch. One floated onto Charley's ear and Amy's hair was covered with them.

The chopper landed. A door opened and stairs unfolded. The first person out was a woman in pink and lavender robes. Next came a man with his head shaven except for a long, thin braid that grew from a patch on his crown. Then a small figure in white suddenly appeared. A hush fell over the crowds and then an immense Ah yee rolled across the land as the trim figure in a stylishly cut white suit raised her hands in a gesture of prayer and bowed to the people.

Charley stood fascinated. Pahata Ra moved through the crowds with a phalanx of robed people. Within the rainbow drafts of their diaphanous flowing robes and scarves she was the still white center. Her own motion seemed to be a kind of apparent motion, or what astronomers call the proper motion in which celestial bodies because of their apparent position in the sky move so slowly that they give the illusion of changelessness. So it was with Pahata Ra. She moved but appeared to remain stationary and not to walk within the phalanx of aides with their wafting, constantly shifting draperies.

She nodded, she smiled. The crowd stilled. A few deep sighs were heard. A woman swooned behind Charley and had to be carried out. The Guardians of the Petal Way remained kneeling all along the carpet of flowers. Pahata Ra would occasionally stop, bend over, and touch one on the shoulder in a special gesture.

Charley and Amy and Barbara were standing at this time directly behind a kneeling guardian. Pahata stopped. The phalanx opened slightly so she could move toward the guardian. Charley had a very close view of her now, at least the top of her head and the curved back as she bent over to bless the guardian. Her hair was a neat blond cap, short and cut at an angle over her ears. With her index and middle finger she touched the shoulder and the nape of the neck of the kneeling woman. Then she looked up directly at Barbara and Amy. Charley felt his heart skip a beat and his throat went dry. The eyes were terrible. They were not human eyes at all.

# 14

——————— "They were iridescent, Mom! I'm not kidding."

"Iridescent? How can you have iridescent eyes? That's impossible."

"Contact lenses. Amy told me so. She always wears them. Nobody's ever seen her without them."

"Gads, it's sounding weirder and weirder."

"You haven't heard anything. Did I tell you about Atlantis?"

"Oh God!" Archie groaned. He propped himself up in the sleeping bag. Charley had just returned from Rancho Radiance and had come into their tent to report the coming of Pahata. He'd gotten back late. Calista had been slightly worried, although Ralph had said there would be a lot of festivities and it might be late. But the more Charley told her of the bizarre goings on the more concerned she became.

"So they actually do believe she is a God, then, and not just a channeler of this Lamata Ra?"

Charley had just finished the story of Atlantis and the divine minerals from which Pahata had derived her deep-degree resonator as an early inhabitant.

"Well, it gets a little complicated. Because basically they believe that every one is a sort of co-God with God. But she's just a little bit more of a God. That's what David Many Hearts keeps telling Amy's mom."

"What?" Calista asked.

"If you don't see me as a God, then you don't see yourself as a God and that's the whole idea of all the therapy they do—to find the God in yourself. That's why she does all this third-eye cleansing stuff every night and every morning."

"Third-eye cleansing?" Calista asked. "Does she wear contact lenses too?"

"Not that kind. It's some visualization exercises. They're trying to get Amy to do them too."

"Who's they?" Archie asked.

"Her mom and David Many Hearts. And she can't bear David Many Hearts. He really is a creep."

He wouldn't get into the stuff Amy had started to tell him about her mom and David Many Hearts, walking in on them and all that. It was so disturbing to Amy. She couldn't even tell him all of it. So she certainly wouldn't want him babbling about it to his mom and Archie.

"Well," said Archie, "do you think any headway is being made with us digging the Los Gatos site?"

"Yep. That is going real well, Archie. The plan is that after the big deal thing tomorrow, the next day you guys are to come over. Barbara has scheduled time with Pahata."

"Sounds like Barbara doesn't have a problem getting to Pahata."

"No problem at all, Mom. Barbara is loaded and she's given Pahata a ton of money and stock and everything."

"Where'd she get the money?"

"Her parents are rich, but she's married and divorced a lot of rich guys. Not Ralph, though. He just sold insurance or something. Amy said she married Ralph when she was in her super-straight suburban-mom phase."

"Oh God, that poor kid!" muttered Calista. She drummed her fingers on the book that lay open on her chest.

"What are you reading, Mom?"

"*Persuasion.*"

"Never heard of it. Who wrote it?"

"Jane Austen."

"Who's she?"

"Oh, just an obscure English writer of the eighteenth century."

Archie laughed and patted her bare thigh in the sleeping bag. "What's the big deal event tomorrow?"

"The Great Harmonic Convergence—it's happening at power spots all over the world."

"What's happening?"

"Well, Mom, would you believe that these folks think we, earth, is on the brink of shooting out of what they call a 'galactic beam' and being sucked up into cosmic nothingness?"

"Sounds like a black-hole scenario. I'm sure your dad would have found it fascinating," Calista said, her voice edged with sarcasm.

"The only black hole is in these guys' heads. They say that all this was predicted on some Mayan calendar and if thousands of people gather at power spots all over the world and resonate in harmony, saying Om—it's the chant for guiding us back on the track—then all this can be avoided."

"So that's why Archie can't see her eminence tomorrow?"

"Yeah, I mean keeping the planet on track does seem more important."

"Of course," said Archie. "What's the use of digging up a site if oblivion is just around the corner?"

"So everybody is going to be busy saying Om tomorrow?" Calista asked, and yawned.

"Ummm." Archie yawned too.

"Guess I better turn in." Charley started to get up from the foot of their sleeping bag.

"Well, come give me a kiss," Calista said. He crawled over to her.

"You think you better give me one too, Charley?" Archie asked. "I mean in case the harmonics don't work and we spin out of the galactic sea-lanes and never meet again." Charley yelled, lunged at Archie, and got him in a headlock.

"Guys, guys, please, not in bed! How many times do I have to tell you . . . no wrestling inside, especially in bed!"

# 15

Spinout had been avoided and business was brisk. There was indeed a festive atmosphere as people hawked a variety of New Age items ranging from crystals to Tibetan bells and various oils. Stalls had lined the road leading up to the compound. Calista and Archie now stopped to observe a man supine on a table balancing bowls on his stomach. There was a sign above the table: Applied Scientific Harmonics Center. A few people were gathered and another man spoke. "These are pure quartz crystal bowls. Now, as we know, quartz crystals reflect macrocosmic universal energy patterns within their microcosmic structure. Each structure, however, has tonal differences. We can actually hear the sounds and feel the vibrations, the tonal character of these different structures, and we can absorb them most directly by placing these bowls just beneath the solar plexus. The bowls then become crystallographic resonating chambers and by filling them with water as we have done here and then ringing them with a small mallet . . ."

"We got to go, guys." Charley came up. "Amy's mom is waiting to take you in."

"Okay. Which way?" Archie asked.

"Follow me."

They entered the main building of the compound.

"Nice," Calista said as they walked into a lobby area with a soaring free-standing fireplace. The rainbow motifs had been damped down. Rock, stainless steel, glass, and quartz crystals were the primary materials. They'd obviously hired a designer, and it was well done. There were two tables set up in the central part of the lobby with architectural models of buildings to be constructed at Rancho Radiance. On the wall were master-plan drawings for future development of the land, which included housing, a holistic arts center, and an amphitheater. Calista was studying the drawings when Barbara Stanton came up.

"Quite impressive, isn't it?" Barbara said.

"I should say." Calista nodded. "What's this over in the corner?" She pointed to what appeared to be a cluster of silos on the drawing.

"Oh, those are mechanical-function things—a water-filtering station and I guess that's just a water tank. I'm not sure."

"Why do they have to filter the water out here?" Calista asked.

"Ugh! Have you ever tasted the water out here on the ranch?" Calista shook her head. "It's awful."

"The water in town's okay," Archie said, walking up. "You got trouble out here?"

"It doesn't have any carcinogens or anything like that. We had it tested. I don't quite understand it, but I guess it comes from an old system put in years ago. It's just murky and tastes lousy."

"Does all of your water come from that old system?" Archie asked.

"I guess so," said Barbara.

"That's odd, but I guess you are pretty high up here and can't tie into the town system that easily. You're right, though, that water is murky, and when the town system runs low they feed into it from the old one and you can taste the difference."

"Most of us have our own filters now, and in the commissary they have filters on all the faucets, but it's very inefficient, so one of the first things is going to be a very elaborate filtering system for the whole place."

"Oh," said Calista.

"We better be going," Barbara said. "This way." Looking over her shoulder, she went on, "Now you understand that these audiences are always two-part affairs. In the first part she channels Lamata Ra. There will be about one hundred people there for that part. In the second part, well, that is the time for special requests, and you go into the inner chamber. Calista can be there for the first part. And then Archie will follow Swami Ben-ji into the inner chamber. Now, Archie, I haven't told her that much. I've only said that you are a distinguished archaeologist and have dug in this region for years and the locals consider you a friend and neighbor. You should explain about the carefulness of your dig and all that stuff you were telling me about backfilling. And while he's doing that, Calista, I thought maybe you'd be interested in coming with me to the Moon Lodge."

"The Moon Lodge?"

"Yes, it's a part of the Wise Woman Lodge—women exploring dreams, structuring dream sequences, holistic journeys. . . ." Barbara's voice seemed to blur into a white noise of tired catch-phrases—New Age sound bites. Well, if she couldn't go with Archie to the inner chamber, why not the Moon Lodge?

. . .

They were now standing in a large room. Calista smelled a heavy, sweet scent, hardly a subtle fragrance. It seemed to be coming from a woman behind her. As in so many orthodox religions, the men and women had been separated. Charley and Archie sat in chairs on one side of the room to the left of a natural rock platform that was in the center. Barbara, Amy, and Calista sat in a section to the right. It was not long before a gong was struck that reverberated throughout the room. Then there was a beautiful sound, a silvery cascade of bells. The Guardians of the Petal Way entered carrying a small carpet of flowers that they placed in front of the stone platform. Calista felt Barbara tense beside her and her breath grew shallow. The lights dimmed and without any further fanfare a small white figure walked out from behind the stone platform. She mounted the two steps and moved toward a stone bench that had a cushion on it and a vase of lilies at either end. Her movements had been measured and smooth until she sat down. Then there was a break in the rhythm barely perceptible, but something startled Calista about the way she sat down. She felt a shiver within her. There was an odd familiarity to something in her movement, the way she lowered herself onto the bench. What was it? Within the microsecond Calista had perceived something familiar but unexpected.

She had a clear view of Pahata. The features were chiseled— a sharp, perfect nose that tilted up just slightly, high rounded cheekbones over which those eerie eyes gazed out at the audience. Lucky Charley had warned her about the eyes. But Calista found them more offensive than strange, the mirrored sunglasses that permitted the wearer to look out and prevented the rest of the world from looking in, therefore presenting a basic inequality in rights of access. And after all, the eyes were supposedly the windows of the soul. There was the presumption here that one person had a right to privacy and access while the other person did not. The one with the glasses, or in this case the contact lenses, had the right to probe while hiding herself. No fair, and more important, what was being hidden? Perhaps the fact that there was no soul.

Calista's eyes were riveted on the face. There was something about that face, parts of it, or was it more an inclination of the head? She felt as if she were looking at pieces of a jigsaw puzzle, but what was the picture supposed to be? She had no idea and it was almost as if other pieces from another puzzle had been mixed in. It was as if an old picture, from where she did not know, of something she did not know had been fractured and reassembled into—what?

Calista was so preoccupied with sorting out the fragments of this elusive image that she barely heard the greeting and the blessing. The voice was so soft that one had to strain to hear it. But it was that soft susurrus that finally penetrated her brain. "My God!" Calista whispered. The chiseled contours of Pahata's face melted away. Harriet Levine! Calista clasped her hand to her chest. Impossible, but it was Harriet Levine, her old roommate from Bryn Mawr.

# 16

Barbara Stanton looked at Calista, realizing that something was happening. "I know her," Calista whispered.

Barbara smiled sweetly and whispered, "Yes, we have all known her throughout many of our past lives. It is part of the enlightenment cycle of the Rainbow Bridge to come to this realization."

"You . . . you . . ." Calista was about to say that Barbara didn't understand, but she realized that it would never penetrate. Barbara herself was in a state of near rapture and had grabbed Calista's hand in her joy.

Oh shit! How do you tell someone that you were God's roommate and not on the Rainbow Bridge but at Bryn Mawr College twenty plus years before, and that, in short, Pahata should not be channeling Lamata but Levine—horny old Harriet Levine, who had in her sophomore year urged a still virginal Calista toward "venery." Harriet had referred to herself in that period as a Celebrant of Venery. The first time she had said it Calista thought it had meant a merry deer hunter. Harriet had screwed around like crazy, and now, well . . . it did indeed look as if she were screwing the world.

The spirit of Lamata had been summoned.

"I, Lamata Ra, am a sovereign entity. Having lived long, long ago, I have never died but became an ascendant spirit seeking out inspired vessels for my force in Pahata Ra. It is through Pahata Ra that I seek to share my essence with you. Together we build the Rainbow Bridge that will lead to a collective ascendance of consciousness into the spectrum and onto the plane of freest energy. . . ."

Good grief, this was not to be believed! Calista looked across the room toward Archie. If she could only signal him in some way—but his eyes were fixed on Pahata, and old Pahata or Lamata was blabbering on.

"You, each and every one is very important to me. . . ."

I'll say, thought Calista. I drove you to and from that darned abortionist after your herbal douches failed! The crap I put up with from you! Bringing all those guys back to our suite. Oh, it was gross. Not once but twice Calista remembered walking in on Harriet. And Harriet was so disgusting about it all. Going into graphic detail about the relative merits and sizes of their anatomies. There had been one that she called Firehose! Calista couldn't stand it very long and had finally bailed out as a roommate and taken a much inferior room in a much less pleasant dorm. But it had been sheer bliss after one semester with Harriet.

"Fifty-five thousand years ago in my second cycle of ascendancy as an inhabitant of the port city of Gunai, I walked the cobbled streets. . . ."

Calista's eyes opened wide. Since when were there cobbled

streets, let alone port cities, 55,000 years ago? Harriet! For Christ's sake what happened to all that ancient history we all learned? Calista thought of her own high school teacher of ancient history, Miss Krementz. She must be turning in her grave if she was hearing stuff like this. A collective grave turning for all old teachers of ancient history! All those lessons about Mesopotamia and Ur, the Fertile Crescent, and the first real cities—5,000 years ago, not 55,000! Calista looked across the room and wondered if all these people could really swallow it. For the most part, the followers of Pahata were very middle-class people. Archie was not swallowing it. He had a look of gentle bemusement.

Pahata was going on about the Gunai school of hard knocks—poverty, war, pestilence, voyages in reed boats, enlightenment, universal love, the radiating deep-degree resonating crystal buried within the first quadrant of the lost continent of Atlantis that emanated its crystal waves of energy. It was these waves that engulfed the sacred island of something or other—Marique! Marique! Wasn't that the island that Princess Margaret went to? No, it was Mustique, that's right. Holy cow! Calista thought she'd never heard such a crock. But how was she going to get to Archie and tell him before he went to the inner chamber for part two? And if Pahata was anything like her former self she'd probably try to . . . oh, Lord. If Harriet Levine laid one horny finger on Archie, well, get ready to go to another plane, Pahata!

Calista barely listened to the rest of what Pahata was talking about in her trance, she was so busy trying to figure out what to do. She caught fragments of stuff—stuff about little villages, great wars, merchants, donkey carts. Unbelievable that people were swallowing this malarkey as a description of life 55,000 years ago. Perhaps she should not dwell on the fact with Barbara that she had known Pahata in the previous and more recent incarnation of Harriet Levine. But she certainly did want to tell Archie. How would she ever get to him before the second session? It did not look hopeful. The session was drawing to a close. Pahata was coming out of her trance. Lamata, the sovereign entity, had ceased to be present within her body. Calista felt herself being shepherded out of the room with the others. She looked back. Archie was being ushered forward toward the rear of the room behind the stone platform. Suddenly at her elbow she felt a light touch. It was Charley. "How'd you like those ancient cities?" she said under her breath.

He whispered in her ear:

> *"Mumbo Jumbo*
> *"Christopher Colombo*
> *"I'm sitting on the sidewalk eating bubble gumbo."*

The poem had been a favorite of Charley's when he was very young.

# 17

Calista could not wait to get out of the Moon Lodge. First of all the lady with the heavy scent, a certain Loy McClure, was the "facilitator." Facilitator seemed to be a favorite word of these people. Apparently it had less authoritarian connotations than the word "teacher," although from what Calista could gather from Charley, David Many Hearts was a pretty heavy-duty authoritarian in spite of being called a facilitator. Loy, however, was not. Still, it was just not Calista's cup of tea to sit around and discuss menses cycles, orgasms, and constructive masturbation to raise the pitch of ovarian and gonadic vibrations. Loy taught something called the Harmonics of Love. "She is fabulous!" Barbara whispered in her ear. "I can't tell you how liberating it has been for me sexually to learn and practice some of her techniques."

I bet! thought Calista. Gads, she couldn't take any more. For one thing, the scent was getting to her. She had found out that it was a love oil, Loy's own blend that she bottled and sold. Calista was terribly uncomfortable.

"My own sexual growth began, as I was saying the other day, when I stopped doing those movies and began to explore other avenues."

"What movies?" Calista whispered to Barbara.

"She used to do movies—uh, Russ Meyer, you know. . . ."

"I found out then that my real genre was what I came to call the sexual pastoral and with my two partners Alex Debrette and Felix Soltan—oh, as a matter of fact, that is a funny little aside. People started to call our films double X-rated because of Alex and Felix's names both ending in X." The women in the Moon Lodge laughed hard at this. Calista did not. "Anyhow, back to the sexual pastoral. I think the one we viewed last week helped us all feel a lot better about touching ourselves and sharing this touching with others. . . ."

Oh my God, thought Calista, how am I going to get out of this? "This week I want to show you another film made right here on Rancho Radiance at one of the power spots and we shall try to use the quartz crystal bowls. In a few minutes I shall demonstrate how we can place the bowl on the pubis." Calista's mind was racing. She saw an image of herself raising her hand. "Pardon me, I'm a very repressed person. I find this excruciatingly uncomfortable. If you will excuse me."

"Now if we can get ready." The lights in the room had begun to dim. Women started peeling off their clothes. Calista stood up to leave.

"Oh, don't leave, Calista. It's so interesting. You don't have to feel pressured at all."

"Oh, heavens!" Loy was saying. And began walking toward Calista. She was stark naked. She had perfect breasts and a completely shaved pubis that seemed to glisten with oil. The heavy sweet scent seemed to engulf Calista. "We don't want anyone to feel uncomfortable. It is not necessary that you take off your clothes."

"I know. That's why I thought I would leave."

"Oh, we don't mind, do we sisters, if one of our own remains clothed?"

"No!" A chorus of female voices rose up in the dim light.

"Well, you might not mind, but I do," Calista said firmly. Was it like the mirrored sunglasses or Pahata's contact lenses where one remained safely hidden while peering into another's soul?

They had dimmed the lights for the film and it seemed to take Calista forever to thread her way through the naked women on the floor and make her way toward the exit. Just as she reached the door the last number of the film leader flashed onto the screen and when she looked over her shoulder briefly she saw the opening shot. It reminded Calista of those car advertisements photographed in Monument Valley, where the gleaming red Chevrolet Caprice or Toyota was poised at the edge of a sandstone cliff backlit by a setting sun. Only this time it wasn't a Toyota. It was a large ass, legs spread slightly to reveal from this posterior view a glistening vulva. All this was backlit by a low-angle, very low-angle, sun, for the person was crouched on her knees in the desert sand. A less than subtle saguaro cactus hovered in the background.

# 18

She could tell from a distance, just by Archie's posture, that the meeting had not succeeded.

"No dice?" she said as she approached.

"Barely a roll," Charley answered before Archie. "So where do we go from here?"

"Let's discuss it on the ride back. I want to get out of here." Archie spoke tersely.

"Me too," Calista said.

"The Moon Lodge didn't do it for you, huh?" Archie looked up.

"Hardly." She paused. "And I've got to tell you guys something that's going to blow your minds."

"Yeah?" Archie looked directly at her.

"Yeah, but I can't talk about it here."

"I've got something too that would best be discussed off premises," Archie said. "Come on, let's go." He put his arm around her shoulders and the three of them began to walk toward the truck.

From the second floor of the main building a drapery stirred as a white figure pulled it back slightly to watch the three people leave. Her white gown was barely discernible from the deep folds of the curtains.

Below, in the stifling midday heat, Calista shuddered, turned, and looked back at the building.

"What's wrong?" Archie asked.

"Nothing . . . nothing," she said quietly. But she had a sense that Harriet Levine knew she was there.

"So who wants to go first?" Archie said as he drove out the gates of Rancho Radiance and onto the dirt road.

"Well, why not you," Calista said. "What's her objection? Why can't you dig the site?"

"The same old gobbledygook . . . disturbing ancient spirits, dishonoring Native Americans. All the stuff about taking bones back to white men's museums—you know, one part politics, two parts mysticism, lots of filler. It all adds up to a New Age meatball with a nutritional quotient that is decidedly below the minimum daily requirement."

Calista was perplexed by the offhand manner in which Archie delivered this news. On one level he didn't seemed disturbed at all, but then she caught a grim set to his jaw as he finished. "So what's your news?" he asked.

"Brace yourselves." She was sitting in the window seat and Charley was between them. She turned toward them both so she could see their expressions.

"What?" Charley asked.

"What would you say if I told you that I was God's room-mate . . . at Bryn Mawr twenty-one years ago?"

"What?" both Archie and Charley said.

"What are you talking about, Mom?"

"Yeah, Mom?" Archie echoed.

"Pahata Ra is Harriet Levine."

"Who . . . wh . . ." The air in the cab of the truck swirled with half-articulated interrogations.

"It's her. I know it. I'd recognize her anywhere despite the plastic surgery."

"She's had plastic surgery?" Charley asked.

"Yeah, a nose job and something done to her cheeks."

"Which set?" Archie laughed.

"The most visible ones." But Archie's little joke stirred some-thing in Calista. A trigger pulled in some dim recess of her brain, and there was an explosion of images—cheeks . . . fannies . . . asses . . . hairy asses . . . "That asshole!" she shrieked.

"Who asshole?"

"What asshole?"

"Stop the car!" she cried. Archie pulled over to the side of the road.

"You know. What's his name?" Calista was slamming the heel of her hand against her forehead as if trying to jiggle out the name she was searching for.

"Who?"

"Swami Ben-ji Prem La."

"What about Swami Ben-ji Prem La?" Charley asked in a soft voice.

"Leonard Gittelman," Calista said emphatically.

"Leonard who?" Archie looked totally perplexed. "Calista, can we take this from the top? Pahata Ra is Harriet Levine, your erstwhile roommate from Bryn Mawr, and Leonard Gittel-man . . .? Who's that and what's his connection with Swami what's his name and Harriet?"

"Don't say erstwhile. The word has a nuance of nostalgia and in no way am I feeling nostalgic about Harriet Levine. I couldn't wait to get rid of her as a roommate. And the straw that broke the camel's back, pardon the pun, was Leonard Gittelman humping her in the middle of the living-room floor when I came back one night." She glanced at Charley. "Sorry, dear, but I'm sure you've heard worse."

"You mean that Swami guy and your old roommate—doing it? Oh God, he's so gross!"

"We're certainly not talking refined here. Right in the middle of the living-room floor. She didn't even have the decency to take him to her bedroom."

Charley was still saying "Gross," while Archie was laughing over Calista's barb. "What are you talking about, Cal? I'm not following this at all."

"Look, Harriet Levine was my roommate for one semester, my sophomore year. I hated her. I didn't realize I was going to hate her so much. It had started out that it was going to be three of us rooming together, but then Clare got mono. Lucky duck! And I was stuck with Harriet, who was not only the horniest thing on campus and slept with every guy on the eastern seaboard but pontificated endlessly about sex and all her sexual experiences. Remember I told you once I had a roommate who had slept with Jerry Rubin and Abbie Hoffman? That to her that was being a sixties radical?"

"Where does Leonard Gittelman come in?"

"Right in our living room! You know when I saw him that day in the town council meeting in Red Forks I thought he looked familiar. I just couldn't place him. And then just a minute ago when you said 'cheeks'—oh God, how graphic do I have to get here?"

"I think we get the picture," Archie muttered.

"Oh, please! I want to puke. But I had seen his face on previous occasions. Needless to say I have tried, and until now thought successfully so, to obliterate these images. Hardly inspirational to a children's book illustrator."

"So they were lovers?" Archie said.

"Let's not sully the word. They screwed, and now they seem

to be together again. Whether they're screwing each other is immaterial."

"Right." There was an emphasis in Archie's voice that caught Calista.

"What do you mean by right?"

"Well, it just seems that a lot of other people are getting screwed around here"—he paused—"hardly leaving time for them to screw each other. But tell me one thing. What did this Leonard Gittelman do back in those days?"

"Oh, he was just a student, graduate student at Columbia. He was a statistics major, I think. I remember hearing that he went to work for some major poll-taking operation."

"Such skills might come in handy . . . when organizing a religion, especially in the start-up phases."

"Especially if you're not really God," Charley added.

Calista pulled back a moment and looked at Charley. She sensed that he had just said something very profound. The shadow from his Red Sox cap slashed across his face, and his skateboarding T-shirt with its acid colors was streaked with the red dirt of the desert. Not quite Martin Buber, but the notion of God and statistics was a heady one even when delivered from under a baseball cap.

"So Pahata Ra was your roommate. Unbelievable!"

"I know, and it doesn't say much for Bryn Mawr either. I mean, my gosh, all that crap about cobbled streets fifty-five-thousand years ago. Her misinformation is monumental and her knowledge of history is one big black hole—abysmal. And these people buy it."

"Literally," Archie replied. "They need to buy it."

"That's what I don't understand. Is this what Joseph Campbell talks about—that spiritually we have become so impoverished, so anemic in terms of ritual and transformational experiences that we are driven to these K Mart gurus?" Archie chuckled. "And when she wasn't talking about cobbled streets and reed boats and the hard life in Gunai, or whatever it was called, she was blathering on in these vague generalities. Listen, if I were a spirit and came back fifty-five-thousand years from now . . ."

"Yes?" Archie leaned over the steering wheel and turned slightly toward Calista.

"Yeah, Mom, as you were saying, if you were a spirit and returned fifty-five-thousand years from now?"

"Well, I think people would want to talk about more practical things, and I would have a few questions too. Like for starters, how come there is still a civilization? And looking back thirty or fifty thousand years I'd have a few questions very specific for old Lamata too. Hell, I don't care about cobbled streets and universal love. Let's get down to brass tacks here."

"What were the brass tacks fifty thousand years ago?" Charley said.

"You know all that stuff that what's-her-name wrote about in *Clan of the Cave Bear?* Is it true? Did women get to hunt alongside their men or not? Was it really nookie in exchange for food?"

"The old Pleistocene prostitution hypothesis," Archie offered.

"Is that what they called it?"

"Some high protein in exchange for sex and a chance to perpetuate your genes."

"Well, that's the name of the game—getting your genes out there. Although I do think at Rancho Radiance we're dealing with some pretty low proteins if they can swallow all this crap from Lamata or Pahata. And what do they pay for an audience?"

"Four hundred dollars, Amy says," Charley offered.

"We didn't have to pay that, did we?"

"No, Mom. I told you, Amy's mom can get friends in free. She's given so much money to the operation she has a few privileges."

"But for four hundred dollars they swallow all this B.S. about harmony, love, unity. There are so many more interesting questions—how did people live, raise their kids? Is it true about the missionary position? Remember Rae Dawn Chong in *Quest for Fire*—face-to-face nookie for the first time. And what did people think was funny back then? I always have wanted to know what made a caveman laugh."

"Maybe the missionary position," Archie interjected.

"You know, I think you could learn more from Mel Brooks and his 'Two Thousand Year Old Man' routine than from Lamata Ra!" Calista sighed. "What are we to make of all this? And, look, you certainly didn't get far with the Los Gatos thing."

Archie shifted in the driver's seat a bit as if trying to get a kink out of his back. He shoved his sunglasses up onto his forehead, then turned to Charley and Calista. "I'm worried, guys, and it's not about not being able to dig Los Gatos."

"What's it about, then?" Charley asked.

"I'm worried about Tonk and I'm worried about Claudie Perkins."

"What does that have to do with digging Los Gatos?" Calista said.

"That's what I'm trying to figure out and I guess that's why I'm worried."

"Do you think there's some connection between their disappearance and Los Gatos?" Calista asked.

"I sincerely hope not, but . . ."

"But what?" Calista asked.

"I don't know. I think I maybe want to have one more look around. Want to go on a hike, Charley, tomorrow afternoon?"

"Sure."

# 19 ——————— "I don't know, Charley. This
might be totally fruitless. The old geezer's probably bought the farm."

Archie and Charley were winding down a narrow defile. Archie paused, sat down on a rock, and took off his pack. "Beer break," he announced and reached into the pack for a beer and then handed a Coke to Charley. They popped the lids. Archie gazed around, his eyes scanning the steep walls of the canyon. "Maybe it's not such a tragedy to die out here in this desert country when you are almost ninety years old and it is the place that you love." Archie immediately regretted saying this. It was a hard concept after all for a kid to accept, especially a kid like Charley, whose father had died alone in the desert.

The official search for Tonk had been called off the day before. But Archie, when he had decided to go out for one more day, had headed off toward the northeast into a region that he felt had not been as thoroughly covered as Tonto Wash and Canyon Diablo territory.

They resumed their course after the beer break and had been following the narrow path that twisted like a dusty red ribbon through the sagebrush. Archie was a few paces in front of Charley when he stopped and crouched. This was not remarkable. Archie often did this. He saw things ordinary hikers did not. He could distinguish within a fraction of a second a rock fragment that had been worked by an ancient flintknapper, even if it was just a core from which a flake had been struck, from an ordinary rock touched by nothing except natural forces of erosion. Charley marveled at this ability of Archie's. Charley felt like a blind man in comparison, because for Archie whole narratives of the earth and its people melted out of the terrain from the scantiest of fragments. Charley cringed when he thought of the clues, the artifacts, the fragments of the story that he walked by or crushed under his boots. Archie's was an ability he envied and wanted to acquire.

So far, all he could do was look straight ahead and think, Well, there's a sedimentary rock and about forty million years of wind and rain have carved it into something that looks like a teapot. Archie, on the other hand, could walk across an outcrop up to the base of a rock shelf and within five minutes tell you that it had been a hunting shelter five thousand years ago, that piñon nuts had been ground there, and that it had been a station for manufacturing small projectile points, or arrowheads, and that there must have been at one time some trading with peoples of the California Gulf or Pacific Coast from the evidence of a tooled shell bead.

"Okay," Archie said rising. "We've got something here. Come up here, Charley, and stand right there," he said indicating with his hand but not turning around to look at Charley. His eyes were still trained on the ground. Charley did not know quite what to expect. This was not the usual way Archie announced artifact finds or evidences of a possible site. "See this?" he said, pointing directly down to the ground in front of him that looked to Charley for all the world like bare ground. There was not even a pebble. "Looks bare, doesn't it?"

"Yep."

"Too bare," Archie said. "The whole path has been this way for the last several yards, and if you look really close,"—he got out a magnifying glass—"you'll see that it's been covered over, brushed over, to be exact, with some juniper."

"Juniper?" Charley said.

"Yes, and you may note that there isn't any around here. We're not high enough for it. We're in what botanically is called the Lower Sonoran, below thirty-five hundred feet. We've got to go another thousand feet uphill until we get to where the juniper grows in the Upper Sonoran. That's where this juniper whisk broom came from."

"Juniper whisk broom? I'm not following this, Archie."

"Somebody came over this path with a fistful of juniper branches and wiped out the tracks. Somebody who didn't want to be followed. I started noticing the needles from the juniper way back. They didn't belong and the track just seemed too clean."

"So?"

"So, it's been pretty freshly done and that person might still be out here not wanting to be found."

"Do you think it's Tonk?"

"Well, I can't quite figure it out. Why wouldn't he want to be found?"

"This is getting a little bit weird," Charley said.

"I'll say. Unfortunately, I don't think we have time to pursue it anymore right now. It's going to be dark soon and we've got to get back."

"Why? We can find our way back in the dark. I've got a flashlight."

"Naw. Your mom will worry."

"I don't think she will. She was so ticked about her old roommate being God, you know, I think it was kind of a distraction."

"What's there to be ticked about?"

"Well, not ticked exactly, but she was talking about writing her a letter or something."

"Hmmm." Archie rubbed his chin and wondered how exactly one did write a letter reminding God that she had at one time just been your old roommate. He was sure that Calista would find a way. This must be small potatoes for a master storyteller and illustrator like Calista.

# 20

Amy's eyes began to well up and deep within her chest something squeezed like a vise.

"Just trust me," David Many Hearts was saying.

She really had to keep her wits about her. She did not want to cry and she could not just say she didn't trust him, although she didn't. Not for a minute. People you could really trust never had to say "trust me." That had been Amy's experience. And people who had to say it wouldn't take no for an answer anyhow. So where did that leave you? Back at square one.

"It's not a question of trust," she replied unsteadily.

"What's it a question of, then?" David Many Hearts took a step closer to her. He was not wearing much—no shirt, and for pants one of those dumb oversized diapers that the men wore when they meditated.

"It's a question of I don't want to do it."

"Do it!" David chuckled. "Amy! Amy! Amy! You sound straight out of Scarsdale, straight out of the fifties, for God's sake. You can't even say the word. Your system of denial is so elaborate that your tongue is forever tied. You are becoming a mute. You are caught in a web, a snare of guilty feelings typical of your class and upbringing. I just want to help you work through all that. Amy, you are a beautiful wonderful person. You have an extremely high energy level, your magnetic resonance is astounding. I felt it that day, the day of your naming, Rainbow Da."

Amy was looking at his diaper. Something moved underneath it. *This guy has a hard-on and he's trying to rape me first with words.* Suddenly she was angry.

"It's a crock, David! Charley Jacobs proved it. He took the Time Slicer out there and that place doesn't have any more electrical charge or vibrations than Cleveland, Ohio. He proved it. It's science." Her face tightened like a wet knot into an expression of defiance.

" 'It's science,' she says!" He spoke in a mocking tone. "And what's science, Amy?"

"Well, what you're doing is not science, but you're trying to pass it off as if it were."

"That's no answer," he sneered.

"That's just your problem. You think you have all the answers. You start with the answers and that is not science. Science begins with questions. You begin with answers."

"Oh, I see that Master Jacobs is truly having an influence here."

"I'm not under anybody's influence. I'm just figuring out how to ask some questions." She paused. "And . . ."

"And?"

"And I'm not afraid of doubt."

"But are you afraid of yourself, Rainbow, of exploring yourself?"

"Would you kindly stop calling me Rainbow! And, no, I am not afraid of exploring myself. But there is more interesting stuff to explore than just me in this world."

"We'll see." With a quick flick of his thumb he loosened the knot at his waist and the diaper dropped.

# 21 ———————————Calista had to play it right.
That was certain. She of course had all to gain and nothing to lose. Her objective was to get permission for Archie to dig the Los Gatos site, although she had to admit that her motives were not totally in the name of science, archaeology, the Smithsonian, or just plain love. Just plain curiosity was driving her too. How the heck had Harriet Levine turned into Pahata Ra? What convoluted mental journey had her old roommate taken to evolve from horny undergraduate to deity? What oversimplifications and delusions of grandeur must one construct in the process? The one thing she promised herself that she would do, and of course this would be the hardest, was to keep an open mind. She couldn't be sarcastic or angry or disdainful. She had to appear open and simply curious.

If this new deity was anything like the old Harriet Levine that Calista remembered, she was very defensive and had a hair trigger whenever her ideas were challenged. She also, as Calista recalled, had shown signs of paranoia in some instances. This could certainly qualify as one—when your old roommate showed up from your less than divine undergraduate days. But then again, Calista vowed she was not showing up to inform Harriet that she was not God; no use in that. This was not to be a confrontation. If anything the reverse—a beseechment exercise. Face it, she thought she was going to plead. Gods usually liked that. That was their thing, so to speak. Being prayed to, asked for things, pled to—supplication. She would outhumble Uriah Heep. Calista told herself all of this.

So how come, after the careful preparation, she was feeling such unhumble rage, and almost from the very start, when she was ushered into the inner chamber where Pahata Ra sat on a beautiful hunk of red rock mounted on a platform. Calista had been informed to remain off the platform, about fifteen feet away in the star of flowers. The outline of a star had been laid out using white chrysanthemums. This was where individuals were to stand for private audiences. Archie had already told her about it from his interview the day before.

Pahata looked up as Calista stepped into the star flower. A thin smile creased her face. "I knew you would come."

"How long did you know I was here?"

"Since Sister Stanton told me about the wonderful family that Rainbow Da had encountered and the mother who was the famous book illustrator." She paused and smiled again. "I've followed your career somewhat. Quite illustrious."

Calista was tempted to say "yours too," but didn't. Instead she spoke quietly. "Then you know about Tom and how he died?"

If she had never spoken of Tom the entire interview might have gone differently, or then again, it might have gone the same way except that she would not have become angry so soon in the course of things. But wasn't it natural to tell someone that you had not seen in years of the large, life-changing events that had occurred, such as the death of one's husband?

Harriet nodded solemnly and then rose from the bench and moved down the steps toward her. She reached out with her hands. They were small and cool and dry. Like a snake's skin, the thought flashed through Calista's mind.

"But, my dear, he did not die."

"What do you mean?" It was at this moment that somewhere deep within her she began to feel the first heat of rage and the humble facade began to disintegrate.

"On the Rainbow Bridge with my spirit guide Lamata, on the

higher plane of crystal reason with the ascended masters of the astral field I encountered Tom."

Calista flared. "Harriet, I find this profoundly offensive," she said, and withdrew her hands from Harriet's.

"My child"—Calista rolled her eyes but Harriet did not seem to notice—"do not let this negative energy of yours interfere. You have always had a volatile nature."

"Harriet! For Crissake, I didn't come here to be lectured. This is starting to sound like a parent-teacher kindergarten conference."

"Look, I know, my dear, that it saddens you to think that your beloved came to me before you."

*You fuckhead!* She clamped her mouth shut and glared into the serene mask before her.

The iridescent contact lenses screened any light of emotion. The eyes, those "windows of the soul" were not human. They were not animal for that matter. Calista had seen more soul in Rambo the hamster's eyes, and yet this jerk was daring now to talk about the soul. Specifically Calista's.

"You are not prepared, dear. Your soul star is not sufficiently cleared of negative effluvia. It is but a dim spark now above your crown." She had tilted her chin up and seemed to be focused on the top of Calista's head with its pile of gray streaked hair clamped with a barrette.

Calista could hold back no longer. "Blaah! Blaah! Blaah!" The words exploded from her mouth with scalding disgust. So long, Uriah, she thought. Even the ascended master seemed to shrink a bit.

"What?" Harriet drew back.

Calista took one step forward and leaned in close. Harriet stepped back out of the star of flowers and hit the bottom step of the platform. She fell down, not hard, but rather gracefully, into a sitting position on the second step of the platform. Calista was now looking down on Harriet, who looked up at her.

"Harriet, don't talk to me about souls. It makes me nauseous."

"It's your soul-star, dear." Was there a slight tremble in the chin. "You must nurture it . . . Tom . . ."

Calista leaned forward closer. Her face was red now, streaked with rage. In a low voice, with crisp enunciation, she began to recite the words:

> "*Mumbo Jumbo*
> "*Christopher Columbo*
> "*I'm sitting on the sidewalk*
> "*Chewing bubble gumbo.*"

She delivered the nonsense poem carefully with eloquent deliberation.

# 22

This was simply not happening, Amy told herself. But David Many Hearts was moving toward her in a crouched position, getting ready to lunge. She saw his muscles coiled and ready to release. The thing between his legs was erect. She would not look at it. She saw those muscles in his shoulders spring-tight. It reminded her of something else— the tension before the gun. The breathing was the same too, shallow and rhythmic. How many track lineups had she been in hearing these vaguely similar sounds. He was strong, but she was fast. She knew it. Quickness was not all muscle, nor was it merely reflex. It was partly in your head. She knew that. She could see her own quickness flashing in her mind. She could explode! And she did. It was so fast that when it happened it took no thought. Her mind was a blank. She did it the same way she exploded off the mark in the junior varsity broad jump. She burst forward in a sleek, arcing leap, her arms and legs extending, reaching beyond the imaginable. It was an unbelievable moment. She was airborne and David Many Hearts stood stock still in his tracks. Then she did something that really stunned him. As if she had all the time in the world, she turned around and in an effortless move of her arm swept up the loin wrap that lay on the floor and vanished.

Her heart was pounding and after the first flush of her triumphant leap something broke loose inside of her and she felt what seemed like a tidal wave of tears. By the time she reached her family's cabin she was sobbing hysterically.

Her mother was not there. So she spilled out the story to Ralph in disjointed chunks. He sat in horrified silence.

"I don't know what to do, Ralph. I can't stand it here. I just don't know what to do." She buried her head in her hands.

"Well, I know what to do," Ralph said quietly. Amy looked up. There was a resolution in Ralph's voice that she had never heard before. She looked at him now. It could have been a totally different person sitting across from her. His jaw acquired a sudden angularity, his mouth became a firm, harsh line, and his usually mild brown eyes were smoldering. "We are getting out of here, Amy."

"You mean you and me?"

"Absolutely. Your mother and I have decided to separate. I just can't take it anymore either. She is not the woman that I thought she was."

"But if you're separating from her . . . I mean . . ."

"Amy, I am certainly not going to leave you behind. I'm a responsible human being. Even if David Many Hearts had not attempted to rape you, I was planning on going to your grandparents and saying that they should intervene here for your sake. I'm just going to deliver you there myself."

"I think I'd better go."

"I know you should go, Amy."

It felt so good to have somebody calling the shots who really did have her best interests in mind. For too long Amy had had to be the mature one in her family. She was so tired of it. "I've got to say goodbye to Charley."

"Of course, dear."

"Maybe he could come and visit me at Grammy's and Pop's in Santa Barbara sometime."

"I don't see why not. There is still a lot of summer vacation left."

"What are you going to do, Ralph?"

"What do you mean?"

"I mean if you and Mom aren't married and all."

"I think I'll go back to work, for starters."

"That sounds nice," Amy said wistfully. "That's the way it was when we first met you."

"You're right. Come on, let's pack up."

## 23

At the finish of the poem Harriet sighed. "Okay, Cal. What do you want?" she said in a weary voice.

Her first defenses seemed to be down. Now if she would only take out those damn contact lenses! Calista sank onto the step next to her. No use trying to stand over her. "Look, Harriet." Calista's voice was warm now and intimate. "I don't know what this shit is you're into."

"Talk about being offensive, Calista! This is a religion, you know."

"Okay, sorry. Listen, nobody needs to know that we were old roommates, that I knew you before all this." She gestured at the rock throne.

"I don't hide things, Calista. They know that I have had previous lives both on this plane and others."

Calista looked at her for a moment. Was it possible that she really believed all this stuff herself? She'd ask about that later. She now had to tell Harriet what she wanted. Harriet had asked her, after all.

"Look, Harriet, all I want is for Archie to be able to dig at Los Gatos."

"I've already told him why that's impossible."

"But, Harriet, that's nonsense. Archie has been digging out here for years with the fullest cooperation of all the people— white folks, Native Americans. He has never had any trouble. As a matter of fact, he has received honors from the Navajo and the Apaches out here."

"But none from the Anasazi."

"Well, there aren't exactly any around to do the bestowing."

"Their spirits are still here and that is the problem." She paused. "Their souls." She said the words almost defiantly.

"Look, Harriet," Calista continued calmly, "for just a minute forget the souls and the spirits."

"I cannot. I am a spirit reincarnate; I occupy a position in the hierarchy of astral souls."

Yes I know, thought Calista, and that's how you met up with Tom on the astral plane. Tell me, has he solved Grand Unification Theory up there? But she contained her thoughts and persevered in calm, even tones. "Okay, perhaps you are. But just for the sake of practicalities, let's not focus right now on spirits and souls, but your problems out here."

"What problems?" Harriet said in a voice tinged with indignation.

"You've got problems, Harriet. People don't like you out here."

"People don't like me!" Harriet threw back her head and guffawed as Calista had never imagined a God or ascended master guffawing. It was the old Harriet laugh. Raucous as hell, just the way she used to laugh when reciting one of her sexual adventures with the Firehose or whomever. "They love me! I've got— what?—five thousand people here this weekend—and by next weekend at the time of the second Astral Ascendancy there will be fifteen thousand. Continental Airlines is offering a package deal to my followers. Three hundred dollars round trip from the East Coast with stopovers in L. A. and San Francisco. I've got

people donating everything from food to port-a-potties. And you
say they don't love me? You're nuts."

"I'm not talking about your followers, Harriet. I'm talking
about the locals."

"The locals?" Harriet said in dismay. "How many locals are
there? Fifty, seventy-five. Most of them on their last legs."

"This is not very compassionate talk for an ascended master,
a religious leader."

"I'm being practical," Harriet said, with emphasis on the last
word.

"Not necessarily."

"What do you mean?"

"I mean that these people have lived here, many of them, for
all of their lives. This is their home. The only home they know.
And you're moving in like gangbusters. Redoing the town."

"Improving the town."

"Changing its name."

"We might not do that. And besides, what does this all have
to do with your friend Archie?"

"Archie is kind of an institution himself out here. The people
like him. They feel honored that he seeks to do his work in their
country. He is an eminent scholar and he pays attention to them
and listens to them and values what they know of this land and
its people. They like that."

"So?"

"So, you're saying no to one more thing that they value."

"Your boyfriend?" Harriet said with a sneer.

"Not my boyfriend—it's the work he does. They value that.
He pays attention to their history. He listens."

"He listens and they love it and now you're saying I'm stopping
this process."

"Well, yes." Calista paused. She then turned around and faced
Harriet squarely with genuine curiosity. "When was the last time
you listened to anybody?"

"I listen to Lamata every day."

Calista bit her lip lightly and contemplated. She felt Harriet watching her.

"You don't believe me, do you?"

"Is that important?"

"No."

"I just can't help but wonder . . ." Calista paused.

"Wonder what?"

"A lot." She sighed. "But, Harriet, how in the hell did you and Leonard . . . ." She saw Harriet jerk slightly. "Yes, I realize that Swami what's-his-name is Leonard Gittelman. I recognize him even with his pants on."

Harriet giggled and her eyes crinkled up into slits of iridescence. It was the first genuine emotion that Calista felt she had expressed. "You still remember that?"

"Yes, unfortunately. His ass was not a thing of beauty."

"You never saw Burton, did you?"

"Burton?"

"You know, the one I called the Firehose."

"Well, no, of course not. I try not to make it a practice of walking in on people while they're copulating. Although it was difficult with you."

"Burton's ass was exquisite. I mean I called him the Firehose for the obvious reasons, but really, his ass!" A soft tone of reverie had crept into Harriet's voice as she recalled some long-gone lover's endowments. "So, what's Archie like?" she said suddenly.

"What do you mean?"

"I mean in bed, naturally. And what does he look like down there. Heavens, he sure is attractive. Do the other parts add up? Well hung, big balls. I always liked big balls. They tickle right behind . . ."

"Jesus Christ, Harriet!" Calista interrupted. My God, she thought, this woman was purporting to be a divine being, an ascended master and asking about balls. "What do you take me for? You think I'm going to sit here and talk about my sex life and give you a detailed anatomical account of Archie?"

"Oh, I forgot, dear." Harriet patted Calista's knee. "You were always very uptight about these things. Very repressed. How long did it take you to shuck your virginity?"

Calista's mouth hung open in dismay. But wasn't this the old Harriet? she told herself. So she shut her mouth and then looked slyly at Harriet. "Too long, according to you, if you remember."

"It was that guy from the University of Pennsylvania wasn't it?"

"Yes."

"And didn't I tell you your art would improve when you started to express yourself sexually, and isn't that when you sold your first picture book?"

"No. It was a few years later, actually."

"You won a Caldecott, didn't you, that big prize for best illustrated children's books?"

"I've won two. The first one about ten years or so ago."

"Oh, that was probably when I was still in the underground."

"Underground? You?"

"Yes, I well . . . it's a long story. I was hanging around with the Weathermen in the early seventies."

"You had to go underground? What did you do, bomb something?"

"No, it turns out that I really wouldn't have had to go. I thought I had to. Thought I was on a wanted list, thought I was maybe in some big trouble."

Could this explain something, Calista wondered, at least in terms of Harriet's skewed values to think that you were on a most wanted list and then to discover you weren't, even if it was the FBI that was doing the wanting? Rejected again?

"Is that when you had the plastic surgery done?"

"The nose then. The rest later. I wasn't really trying to disguise myself. It's just . . ." Her voice dwindled off.

"It's just what?"

"Well, it sounds crazy, but you know plastic surgery can become sort of addictive. You fix a little something here, then you notice another defect there. And it's just so easy . . . you know how to transform yourself. You can just sort of fiddle around with it all."

Interesting, Calista thought. And after she had fiddled around and fixed her face she began with her "soul" and its transformation. But how had she made the leap to godhead? Did Leonard Gittelman have something to do with it, perhaps?"

"How did you meet up with Leonard again?"

"Oh, we'd never really lost contact. You know Leonard was such a nerd. He was going great guns in terms of his statistics stuff. I mean every major pollster was hiring him and marketing firms, but he was still like this nerd. No self-confidence. I helped him a lot sexually. He was eternally grateful for that. But I couldn't do it all, and somehow or other he got into, as they call it, the human potential movement. What he basically saw was not only his own potential but the business as well as the political potential. He started doing some statistical work for himself. Profiles of populations that went for this kind of thing. Actually he did a lot of work for the televangelists and those Christian broadcasting networks."

It was all starting to make sense. Leonard had probably figured out all the statistics. Although the Age of Aquarius had arrived, the full potential in terms of money and power had not yet been tapped. He needed a guru and marketable God.

"So how did you and he get together?"

"Well, I had just emerged from the underground and I had gotten into some transformational therapy stuff and I had . . ." She paused. "Well, if you read my book it's all right there. I had some very startling metaphysical experiences. A spirit guide was revealed to me during a very unusual sexual experience."

Calista would not ask. She assumed it was not with the Firehose. "In any case—I know that you think this is all a crock—but it was real. Very real for me. And I told Leonard about it and he was fascinated. I had, after all, helped Leonard a great deal in the past, and he believed in me and believed in my potential to help others." And he had the demographics down pat, thought Calista. "So that's sort of how the whole thing started."

"The whole thing," Calista said softly.

"And you don't believe it, do you?"

"As I said before, why should it matter to you whether I do or not?"

"I guess it doesn't," Harriet replied.

"I do have some questions, though."

"What about?"

"Well, this Lamata, for one thing."

"Do you want me to summon her so you can ask her directly?" Was she bluffing or what? "No, I think I'll just settle for you."

"Okay, what are your questions?"

How to make this sound like gentle inquiry and not total disdain, Calista thought. "Well, Harriet, with all due respect." Her voice did have a quiet sincerity.

"Yes?"

"Well, I can't help but think that suppose, for example, the tables in a sense were turned. Just try to imagine that my spirit, unevolved as it is, and my dark soul star . . ."

"Your soul star isn't dark, dear." Harriet was slipping back into divine mode with all these "dears." "My child" would undoubtedly soon follow. "An active, undarkened soul star only requires a willingness toward self-improvement."

"I hate self-improvement, Harriet. You should remember that about me. I hate diets. I hate exercise. I'm so sick of Jane Fonda I could puke. Anything that smacks of self-improvement just turns me off. Not that I don't need to be improved."

"That admission is a beginning, my child."

There, she'd said it! Hah! She knew she was right. Oh well, to hell with it, Calista thought, and continued her argument. "Anyhow, as I was saying if, murky spirit and all, I somehow found myself inhabiting somebody else's body thirty thousand years from now . . ."

"Yes? It's not impossible," Harriet said in an encouraging voice.

"Well, I think that I would talk about, you know, a few more concrete things than Lamata talks about, for starters. You know, all this universal love, consciousness, self-awareness."

"Lamata does talk a lot about concrete things—her life in Gunai."

"Okay, hold it right there," Calista said, raising a finger. "I have a problem with that."

"What's your problem?"

"Harriet, you and I both know that fifty-five thousand years ago there were no cobbled streets. I mean really, Harriet, you did get into Bryn Mawr on something. Don't you remember your ancient history course from high school? Every kid in the country probably read that same old text book. Breasted's *History of the Ancient World* or whatever it was called. They did not have streets, let alone towns, fifty-five thousand years ago."

"This was part of the lost continent," Harriet replied. "It was part of another civilization, much more advanced."

"Well, if it was that advanced, how come it vanished without a trace?"

"Because the people lost their faith in the cataclysmic seizure of the Second Astral Ascendancy."

Oh, God, this was useless. She'd try another tack. "Well, look, forget the cobbled streets and all that. Let's get back to the hypothetical situation: if I were a spirit thirty thousand years from now."

"Okay."

"Okay, now you know what my first question would be if I came back."

"No, what?"

"How come there's still civilization, let alone an ozone layer? And what about the abortion issue? Is there still a *National Geographic*? Are the north and south poles vaguely in the same place?"

"Are you trying to say that Lamata does not offer valid information?"

"I'm trying to say that Lamata is being too vague to be convincing or anything except that she is a figment of an imagination, and that anybody could say this stuff. I'm not going to try and dissuade your followers. I have no interests in their spiritual lives."

"Your son does, though," Harriet said quietly.

"Charley? What are you talking about." Something tightened in Calista's chest.

"He's been out there with his little machine trying to prove that the vortices aren't true magnetic force fields."

A chill crept over Calista.

# 24

Dear Charley,

I stopped by to say goodbye. I know this seems kind of sudden but this really gross thing happened. I can hardly think about it let alone write about it. But in any case David Many Hearts tried to attack me. I got away. Remember I told you I was good in track. Well, this time I was brilliant but it wasn't on any track. I can't talk anymore about it. It was just so gross. Anyway Ralph is as fed up with this place as I am and he's taking me to my grandparents in Santa Barbara. I'm including their address and phone number and it would be so cool if you could come and visit. It's really not that far from here. Ralph says it's less than a day's drive.

I'm sorry I didn't get to say goodbye in person but you were out with Archie when we stopped by. Your mom wasn't here either. I just want to say that this isn't really goodbye cause I know we're going to see each other again. So I don't want to get all sloppy, but it's just been so cool knowing you and I think your mom and Archie are just awesome. And just do write to me and try to come and visit. My grandparents are pretty cool for their age and they have this neat lady chauffeur who's really into surfing and skateboarding and she'll drive us anyplace we want to go. And Pop was talking about getting some video game machines for the pool house so we could have a fairly awesome time.

Your Friend,<br>Amy Solomon

"I don't believe this!" Charley said, staring at the note.

"What?" Archie said, looking up from a pottery sherd he was examining with his magnifying glass. They were sitting in the lab tent.

"Amy is gone!"

"Gone? Gone where?"

"To Santa Barbara, her grandparents . . ." He paused. "And you know why?"

"Why?"

"Because that creep David Many Hearts tried to attack her."

"Attack her—you mean as in sexual assault?" Archie said, putting down the pottery sherd.

Charley bit his lip nervously. It was the same gesture, identical to his mother's when she was either frightened or thinking very hard. His luminous gray eyes seemed to grow enormous at this prospect. Archie suddenly felt infinitely sorry for him. This smart-ass, wonderful kid who was a computer genius, who had done as much as any of his graduate students all summer seemed ineffably fragile now, like a distillation of all the innocence in the world. "I think that's what she meant, Archie." He spoke slowly. "She said it was real gross but she got away."

"Oh my God!" Archie rubbed his hand across his eyes. He looked for that instant so old to Charley. Charley was flooded with fear. He stood up and walked over to Archie, grasped him around the chest, and buried his head in his shoulder. He began to cry softly. He didn't know why exactly. He was crying, he guessed, for Amy, but she had escaped. So it didn't make sense exactly. But he was still crying for her. He was crying for her having to be so brave all the time, having to be the responsible one in the family, having to be a track star for a rapist!

"It isn't fair!" he sobbed into Archie's shoulder.

Calista had walked into the lab tent quietly. Archie above Charley's head had tried to give some gesture that would ease her.

"What?" She asked in a quiet voice. Charley did not even hear her question through his sobs.

"Your mom's here, Charley. You want to tell her what happened or should I?"

Charley lifted his head. "Maybe you better, Archie."

"Oh my God," Calista said, after Archie finished explaining what had happened to Amy. "Then that explains one thing!"

"What?" both Charley and Archie asked at once.

"Well, as you might have guessed, while you guys were out searching —I'll ask you about that in a minute—I just couldn't hold back. I went to see my old friend Harriet."

"I told you she would," Charley said, looking at Archie.

"Yes . . . and how did that go?"

"Oh," Calista said with a dismissive wave of her hand, "just about as I expected. I'll tell you all about it, but when I was arriving for my private audience with her shining radiance, or whatever the hell they call her, I was met by a rather strange sight."

"Which was?" Archie asked.

"David Many Hearts trying to make as discreet an exit as possible from a building next to the main one. He was totally nude except for a movie screen that he was literally trying to screen himself with."

"Jesus!" said Archie.

"Do you think that this is when he tried to attack Amy?" Charley asked.

"I don't know," Calista said. "But this is getting bad."

"It sure is," said Archie. He had dug out his pipe and with his Swiss Army knife was jabbing at the old tobacco in the bowl. "I think I know what has to be done," he added, looking up.

"What's that?" Charley asked eagerly.

"I'm going down to Phoenix. I'm getting hold of the D.A. We have two missing persons and an attempted rape."

"Two missing persons—Tonk and who else?" Charley asked.

"Claudie Perkins. Agnes Bessie left word for me that she checked on the only relative that anyone knew Claudie had down in Yuma."

"And?"

"That relative died fifteen years ago in a nursing home in Tucson."

# 25

Archie and Calista headed for Phoenix the next morning. Calista fretted over Charley, and wanted him to accompany them, but he had no desire to endure a long, hot drive and insisted on staying behind to fiddle with the new data base he was writing for cross-referencing pottery sherds from five of Archie's major sites. But by mid-morning a coil had blown on his thermal printer and he was getting bored, to boot, so he decided to quit.

He realized in any case that everything he had been working on all morning had just been a way of not thinking about Amy, of trying to push all that to the back of his mind. But it hadn't worked, and thoughts of Amy and her troubles kept clawing their way to the front of his mind. There was very little he could do about Amy. It seemed to him that it had suddenly become grown-ups' business. Something for Archie and his mom and district attorneys to handle.

There was something else rustling about in the back of his mind. It seemed important. It seemed that there might be something he could do—why, of course! He stopped tapping the keys of the computer. Those footprints, the covered tracks. They had

completely forgotten about them in the flurry of the news about
Amy. Now, there was a puzzle. Charley had begun to think
about it earlier. If Archie said the juniper grew high up and had
to be brought down to cover the tracks, which way was the walker
really heading and what had been his or her origin? He would
have had to have been up high at some point to get the juniper.
Was he or she trying to cover the tracks back up, or was that
person heading down for good and had brought the juniper with
him, trailing it? It would seem impossible to tell which way the
boots had been pointing in a covered track. But it was an interesting question, and one worth pursuing. Why not try to figure
it out?

Nobody was in camp right now, as they were all out at the
old site or on survey hoping to find evidence of what could be a
new site that did not fall under Rancho Radiance's authority. It
wasn't that far, however, to where he and Archie had trekked
yesterday. They had had to park their truck a good ways from
where they had started to hike anyway, as the terrain was inac-
cessible to vehicles, more so than Archie had thought it would
be. So from where they had parked the truck to camp had really
been only a bit over a mile. And then it had been another mile
and a half into where they found the tracks. He could walk that
easily. From where he was right now to that track couldn't be
more than three miles. It was cloudy today. So the heat was not
too bad. That was why the excavation teams planned to stay out
through the noon hour.

He was bored. He wanted to do something. He wanted to
make progress on some front. He grabbed two canteens, stuffed
three oranges and two boxes of Cracker Jacks into his backpack
along with his sling, a sweatshirt, and a rain poncho, just in case,
and set off.

He didn't even feel tired by the time he got to the spot where
Archie and he had discovered the covered track. This time he
began to notice quite a bit sooner what Archie had been noticing

all along the path: it was too clean, too immaculate. He spotted the occasional juniper needle, which indeed looked out of place to him now amid the prickly pear, cholla and beaver-tail cacti. But which way had the person been heading? This was the problem. He was determined to figure it out. If you couldn't find a boot mark pointing in a definite direction, was there something else? For example, did a juniper needle have a front and back end to it, because if it did . . . Charley picked up one of the needles and took out his Swiss Army knife with the magnifying glass, the one just like Archie's that Archie had given him for his birthday.

From high above, well into the Upper Sonoran zone, the crouching figure of Charley was drawn into the thin cross hairs of a telescopic sight.

# 26 _____ "All right, I give ya something

for tracking me here . . . better than those other fellers. . . ." Tonk Cullen muttered to himself, and hunkered down behind an ephedra bush. He had broken off a twig and was chewing on it. His thirst was relieved, and as long as he had to stay up high, away from his water sources, he was sure to keep a twig handy. "Where's the feller that was with you yesterday? He looked like he knew what he was doing."

Tonk lifted the telescopic sight that he always carried with him. He'd taken it off an old 30-0-6 years before and refashioned it for a small, pocket-size scope. He had carried it with him for over forty years. But he couldn't remember that now. He couldn't remember his name, or where he'd gotten the scope, although he recognized how clever the adaptation was and how nicely it fitted into his pocket. But he had not the vaguest idea of who he was, why he was here, and where here was. Oh, it was high desert country, all right. Seemed like home. Seemed familiar, but he just couldn't place it.

All he knew was that there was something closing in on him, some scent of danger all about. And it didn't seem right, because he felt at home in the desert. Always had—whatever "always" had been. It didn't disturb him much that he couldn't remember the details—like his name or what he was doing. He knew the important things—how to find water or make Mormon tea, as he could from this ephedra bush, or where to find mesquite beans, and what cactus had fruit at this time of year, although he couldn't precisely say what month it was.

What did disturb him was this unnamed sense of danger. He'd felt it since—when? Well, whenever it was that he had found himself all cut up in the bottom of the gulch. He still had a lump on his head size of a hen's egg. But he had patched himself up pretty good. He'd found a cream cactus right there, slit it open, and spread its milk over his cuts and bruises. Then, just about as soon as he got himself fixed up and found himself a water hole, he spotted the other two fellers. They was hunting him. He knew it. Next a helicopter came swooping down. Soon it seemed like everybody was out hunting him. So he just holed up. He didn't know why he didn't want to be found. He just didn't. He smelled danger.

Now this young critter—he raised his scope—how dang dangerous could he be? He was almost tempted to—but you never could tell, could you? No, he better just stay hunkered down till this feller left and he could get back to his business, whatever that was.

That was the other thing that kept bothering Tonk. He did have some business to do out here, but for the life of him he couldn't remember it. He had this map folded up in his pocket, but he couldn't figure out what he was supposed to do with it. He just kept staring at the map and not seeing it so good, because his spectacles had got shattered somehow. He could only see through the left lens and it had two big cracks. The right one was gone completely. So he'd take out the map and his glasses and hold that lens up to his eye and study that map. But the map didn't really say anything on it, just showed some kind of routes for something or other. Said "water ordinance" at the top, but what the heck did that mean? He had a feeling, though, that his business out here had something to do with that, and another thing too. But he couldn't remember the other thing either. It just blew through his mind like some pale lavender shadow from some distant and very sweet time. Made him ache a little inside. Jesus Christ, it was hell getting old. Absolute HELL!

"Hell!" The word clanged down the scrubby incline like an old metal pot.

"What?" Charley shouted. He was halfway up the incline. In Tonk's reverie he had completely forgotten the figure in his sights and began mumbling aloud and then shouted. Now he clamped his hand over his mouth.

"Gol-dern fool," he muttered into his hand. There was no hiding now. The kid was nearly there and had spotted him crouching behind the ephedra.

Charley couldn't believe it. "Are you Tonk?"

The old man was silent a moment and Charley saw him slide his eyes up under the bushy gray brows as if he were contemplating these words more as a piece of information than a question.

"What's it to you?" he growled.

"Well, everybody in Red Forks has been looking for Tonk Cullen."

"Wouldn't know him if I saw him. What's Red Forks?"

"Red Forks? You've never heard of Red Forks?" Charley said slowly.

"Naw. What business a fork got being red?"

This was unbelievable. If this wasn't Tonk Cullen, who was it? Charley wondered. Where could he have come from? How could he not have heard of Red Forks? This guy had to be from another planet. Maybe a Merkabah? Charley took a step forward.

"Hold it right there, young feller! I got a thirty-ought-six on you. One more step and the turkey buzzards got themselves a meal and the wind can whistle Dixie through your arsehole."

Why did he like this man? Amazing. Maybe it was just the no-nonsense approach as compared to the folks at Rancho Radiance, but in truth Charley felt more at ease with these homey profanities than with the airy language of harmonic bliss. Maybe he should take a cue from this guy and try the no-nonsense approach, and besides, deep down he just knew this had to be Tonk Cullen. Hadn't they said that he had some sort of seizures at times that could make him disoriented?

"Well," Charley began, "I'm just out here looking for this guy Tonk Cullen, because everyone's real worried. They're sure he's dead."

"He ain't dead," Tonk said emphatically.

"How do you know? You said you never heard of him."

Tonk scratched his head and mulled this over for a minute. Then he stood up slowly, still scratching the back of his head. So he had to push his cowboy hat forward a bit.

"Well, young feller, you got me there." He spoke in a deeply ruminative tone, not as if he were admitting anything, but just as if he were genuinely stumped. He began to move out from behind the ephedra. He looked at the scope in his hand. "Oh, don't worry none. It ain't a gun, just part of one." He began moving down the incline and closing the twenty-foot gap between them. "You see, son, this Tonk Cullen. . . ."

"Yes?"

"Well, the name does ring a bell. . . ."

Holy Jesus, thought Charley, this guy really has gone over the edge.

"And I can't tell you why, but deep down in my gut I don't think your man Tonk is dead."

"No, sir," Charley said quietly, "I don't think so either." He had walked right up to him. "Here, sir." He offered him his canteen. "Would you like a drink of water? And I have an orange in my backpack."

**27**————————"Ecstasy is a new frequency that we are attempting to define." Pahata Ra was saying to a small group of her followers, those who were considered second-degree initiates and whose soul stars had attained a certain luminosity that allowed them to share the vision. They also happened to be those people who had made contributions upward of five thousand dollars.

Barbara Stanton was trying very hard to concentrate on the frequencies of ecstasy but was finding it very difficult. She had returned to Rancho Radiance after a brief trip to the south rim of the Grand Canyon with Pahata in her helicopter, where Pahata had met with a group of New Age paraplegics to join them in some cosmic visualization exercises that were proving quite effective. Barbara always enjoyed these little diplomatic missions. She functioned as a kind of aide and often as press liaison.

But when she had returned she had found Ralph's astounding note. Of course it wasn't true. It was just Ralph's way of getting back at her. He had no understanding of how David, who knew a hell of a lot more about sulky adolescents than Ralph did, was just trying to help Amy understand her conflicting feelings. Rape! How ridiculous. Amy was a pro at exaggeration. David was not in the least attracted to Amy. In the beginning he hadn't even been attracted to Barbara. He had admitted this. But now she had become attractive to him and he to her. She could, however, look at all that objectively. She did not need David. She did not need to have him exclusively and that was the way it should be. He had helped transform her into a truly giving person and she should not hoard her gifts nor bestow them exclusively but rather evenly, with grace and with feeling.

However, it had become increasingly evident to Barbara that her growth, this dynamic unfolding of her higher self could not

continue unimpeded if those closest to her were not also growing.
And although she firmly believed that both Ralph and Amy had
the potential, it would never be realized until they opened themselves up to more experiences. Why would it be so horrible if
David and Amy had had sex? Why should her daughter's first
sexual experience be with some lunk, one of those jocks she hung
around with at high school who would get her pregnant, give
her crabs, or, worse yet, AIDS? Why not go with a gentle healer
of the spirit like David—clean, kind, and the spiritual descendent
of Black Elk, seer of the Oglala Sioux! She had discussed just
this possibility with Loy McClure the evening the three of them
first came together in a harmonic triad of self-pleasuring, truly
one of the most sexually and spiritually incandescent experiences
she had ever had. Oh how she had wanted Ralph to be part of
that! That could have really saved them. Oh well, his loss, not
hers.

The session was coming to a close. Pahata was beginning the
blessing of the Guardians of the Petal Way. At the finish Barbara
saw David and Swami Ben-ji follow her out a side door that led
directly to her private office on the second floor. From the expressions on the two men's faces, it appeared as if there were serious
matters to discuss.

# 28

_____ "I'm sick of everyone telling
me that I have problems." Pahata glared at the two silent men
who stood somberly in front of her. "We've got five thousand
people coming in here this weekend, I've got complications with
the Japan tour, I've got the friggin' Pope on my back." She paused
and pointed a finger directly at David Many Hearts. "And you,
David, you are becoming a royal pain in the ass—why are you

trying to get your rocks off with Barbara Stanton's daughter? Barbara Stanton is a decided bright spot in our fiscal lives these days. That Santa Barbara National Bank stock is starting to move and we're going to be able to expand our Washington state holdings substantially, not to mention here."

"That's just the problem, Pahata," Swami Ben-ji was saying patiently.

"What's just the problem?"

"Here."

"Yes, here," David said. There was an ominous chill in his voice. "That kid Charley Jacobs can cause problems. He *is* causing problems."

"What, with his little machine?"

"The talk is getting out, Pahata. I heard Shinon talking about it to two others. Amy had evidently said something about the experiments to her. You can't afford that kind of talk right now before the Second Ascendancy. . . ."

"Not to mention the other matter," Swami Ben-ji interjected.

"What other matter?" she asked.

"The one you don't like to talk about."

"You mean?" She bent her head in a kind of half nod of inquiry.

The two men nodded back and said "Yes" softly.

"Well, what's there to talk about?" she asked with a blend of naïveté and defiance in her voice that irritated both men. "The search has been called off and . . ." She stopped and looked with sudden alarm at David Many Hearts and then at Swami Ben-ji. "Are you not telling me something?"

"No, no. It's really just a hunch," David said attempting a soothing voice.

"That's not exactly right, David." Swami spoke now.

"I want to hear whatever you have to say."

David sighed. "I was out on the Old Palatki Wash Road yesterday. I saw Baldwin's truck. It struck me as odd. There are no archaeological sites in that direction and this wasn't any area where his students have been doing those ground surveys. I think that officially the search must be off but unofficially some people are keeping it going."

"And what? My God, David, the guy has to be dead. He's ninety years old."

"No body has been found," Swami Ben-ji said.

"But it's been days now. He couldn't survive."

"Well, I wouldn't think so. But on my return I decided to come the back way. There's another road that really leads into the same place. I didn't want to run smack into Baldwin and his troops."

"So?"

"I didn't, but what I did see at the bottom of the Palatki Wash was a figure."

"Christ Almighty, was it him?"

"I couldn't tell. It was getting dark by this time. So this morning I went over to Baldwin's camp. I just thought I might, you know, inquire as if I were interested in maybe continuing the search for another couple of days."

"And?"

"And nobody was there, but there was a note from Charley Jacobs. The long and the short of it was that he had gone out to the area where he and Baldwin had been the day before just to look around for Cullen."

"This kid is becoming a problem," Pahata said calmly. "How much of a chance do you think that the figure you saw was Cullen and what are the odds of this kid finding him?" She looked toward Swami as if he would immediately spout some statistical data.

He shook his head and in an almost avuncular tone began to speak. "I don't know, Harriet, but I think it's a chance we can't take." Pahata drew her lips into a firm line. She listened to Swami especially when he said things in this way.

"What's to be done?" Her voice seemed small.

"We need to get the helicopter and go searching," Swami said quietly.

"And then what, if you find them?"

"Well, we could figure out how much they know," David said.

"No." Swami shook his head slowly but emphatically. "We already know how much Cullen knows."

Pahata Ra and Swami looked quietly at one another.

"I leave the details to you, Leonard," she said in a soft voice, and then turned and walked out of the room.

There was complete and perfect understanding between Pahata and Swami. They didn't even need sex anymore. It was truly heaven on earth and they both knew it.

# 29

"So you honestly think that I'm this fellow Tonk Cullen?"

"Yeah," Charley said. "Me and Archie. . ."

"Archie!" Tonk broke in. "Archie Baldwin!"

Charley nodded, his eyes opened large. "The Smithsonian."

"I know, young feller. You don't have to tell me who Archie Baldwin is. I been helping him with his sites since he was—good God!" The rheumy eyes suddenly blazed. He pushed his hat back. "I am Tonk Cullen. Oh my gracious, it's like I been on a trip and now it's all coming back." He ran his tongue over his mouth as if savoring himself, an old familiar flavor. "And I was pushed, goddammit! No, not pushed—snapped." He slapped his hand against his shin.

"Snapped?"

"Yeah, something snapped me right here, something strung up tight—a trap it was. I know'd it whole time I was falling."

"And you survived?"

"Well, I reckon so. Your'e looking at me, ain't you?"

"Yep." Then Charley asked, "What were you doing out here anyway?"

"Okay, okay," Tonk said in a low voice, and started to look around scrutinizing the terrain. "Now let's take this one step at a time. There are just three things a man has to know."

"Yeah?" said Charley.

"Yeah. He's got to know who he is, where he is, and what he's doing. I got two out of the three. I'm not lost. I'm confused."

"You do?" Charley asked.

"Sure I do. I'm Tonk Cullen, mayor of Red Forks among other things, and I'm out here just east of the Palatki Wash." He paused. "Now all I got to do is figure why in tarnation I'm out here."

Charley waited attentively. Tonk suddenly remembered the map in his shirt pocket. He slapped his hand against the pocket.

Charley was alarmed. "You having a heart attack or something?"

"No!" Tonk barked. "A map." He took the map from his pocket.

"What's that?" Charley asked. It did not seem like the usual kind of map.

"Water-ordinance map. And survey map. Shows all the parcels of land on the old Palatki water system and then the new water company that Clau . . ." His voice dwindled off. Tonk dropped the map in his lap. "Oh my God! Claudie! Claudie! That's why I'm out here."

"Claudia Perkins?" Charley asked.

"Yes, goddammit!" And he sat up straight now as if an electrical current had gone up his spine. "Claudie Perkins had those last parcels of land on the old water system and those goddam Pahatties were using straws to . . ."

Just at that moment they heard a soft staccato thrumping overhead. "Goddam helicopter again!"

"But the search has been called off," Charley said, standing up and shielding his eyes against the noonday sun.

"Somebody must really want to find me," Tonk said and the smell of danger mixed with the dull thrumping sound overhead.

"Jeez, it's a lavender helicopter. . . ." The possible implications began to dawn on Charley.

# 30 _____ David sat glowering in the seat

of the chopper he was piloting. Next to him sat Swami. He knew Swami would take credit for the whole thing and he himself was the one who had alerted them to the danger of this kid in the first place. He was sick of being treated like a junior partner in this operation. But it wasn't only that. He had to face the fact that he envied in a strange way that perfect understanding, that ineffable instant comprehension that Pahata and Swami seemed to share with each other. He envied and feared it because it was a very powerful tool and they could use it in an instant against him, if they so chose. But that would be foolish, and they must realize it. David was an important part of the operation. He had brought in Barbara Stanton, after all, as well as Myra Fenton the actress and Elsa McDougall the sugar cane heiress. Not to mention Sandita Nashim the billionaire arms dealer's daughter. He had literally provided the financing for a good quarter of the real estate empire.

This was in a sense roughly the way the division of labor was supposed to go among the three of them. It had been agreed upon soon after David had come on board. Swami handled the politics and dealing with the real estate, the city council, zoning ordinances for the ranch. David Many Hearts was in charge of recruitment of what they called "special initiates," wealthy women who wanted to find a new way of giving and making their lives more meaningful. That was no junior-partner role, and he was beginning to resent begin treated in this way. He was after all the spiritual descendent of Black Elk. That had been revealed to him almost a decade before, right after he had come back from

Vietnam. He had gone to Kaui with some vets. It had happened in a hanging valley on the island during an LSD trip. It had been an uncanny experience, but he had actually had the identical visions that Black Elk had had before the Battle of Little Big Horn. David apparently had gone down to the beach and drawn some of the same pictures in the sand depicting certain cosmic revelations that Black Elk had drawn. This was verified to him by another vet—George Jameson, who really was a Sioux, the same tribe as Black Elk.

That was how David had come to find himself in the West. It had happened to be at the same time that Pahata was trying to organize an astral ascendancy convocation in the Black Hills region and he proved very helpful to her in her dealings with the Sioux of that area. Thus he had joined the inner circle. But they seemed to have a short memory. Perhaps he should remind them on occasion. After all, just because Swami and Pahata went to fancy eastern colleges was no excuse for them to treat him like some imbecile.

"You know Ben-ji," he began, "sometimes I get the feeling that, well, you know, you folks really don't. . ." Ben-ji stifled a sigh and looked over at David, who kept his eyes focused straight ahead and his hand steady on the stick. They had this discussion about once every six months, it seemed. The jerk should be grateful. Before David had met up with them he'd just been one more Vietnam vet burning his brains out with drugs, and before that just a dumb surfer. He had actually been impotent when they had first encountered him but thanks to Harriet's ministrations he was brought back to sexual life. Then he couldn't get enough of it. That's when they wrote the job profile for him. Stroke of genius. He went from being nothing to being Black Elk's spirit. That came in very handy. Not only that, but they had been very generous with the stupid kid. They had given him as bonuses two thousand shares of UAL, another two thousand of IBM, plus a piece of the action on all the franchises for the Rainbow Holistic Therapy centers as well as a share of the mail-order catalogue business. And of course he got to pork anything that came along, whereas he, Swami, was suppose to maintain an almost virginal image according to the game plan. What the hell was the guy complaining about?

"David," Swami said firmly, "this is not the time to talk about it. We need all your skill with this chopper. I promise you that if this operation is successful I will most certainly sit down with you and earnestly go over any concerns you have. I know you have some concerns. I know they are genuine ones, and there will be time to discuss them. Rest assured, I am more on your side than you might think. After all, it was you and I who confronted Pahata and made her realize how important this . . . this situation is."

Swami saw David's eyebrow lift. That was exactly the response he had anticipated. When there is dissension in the ranks, disgruntled people need empathy rather than sympathy. Wise understanding and a gesture of confidence coupled with a hint that they are on the brink of being brought into a trust can't be beaten. Worked like a charm every time. Swami had been around enough politicians to learn what the good ones did to insure that their ranks closed around them. With that kind of teamwork miracles could be accomplished, even when polls predicted disaster. That, of course, had been Leonard Gittelman's special insight. That was what made him so valuable as a statistician and a pollster, his uncanny perceptions about what statistics really meant, how they could be used and whether they could be trusted or not. Do we serve the statistics or do the statistics serve us? That had been his theme. It was possible to have too much faith in statistics, a kind of blind faith that led to misuse and even abuse of information.

Right now his concern was to get David Many Hearts focused on the issue at hand, make him feel in command. After all, he was the one who was flying this thing. "Okay, David. I want you to run me through the procedure once more before we spot them."

"If we spot them," David answered.

"I think we will. Who the hell is that down there?"

"Oh, Jeez—he's standing right up. Let's buzz in for a closer look." David Many Hearts depressed the collective pitch-control stick between the seats and the chopper cut into a steep dive.

# 31

Charley looked straight up. The helicopter was hovering directly above him, and David Many Hearts was in the pilot's seat! A fat, bald man sat next to him. And then it all happened too fast. There was no time for anything: there was the noise, the hot drafts of tumultuous air lashing about them, and suddenly a tangle of something plummeting down on them. At first Charley thought that part of the helicopter had fallen off. I'm dead. The thought rang clear in his head. But a second later he realized he wasn't dead at all. He was caught, and so was Tonk. Snared like a spider's prey in its web.

"What in tarnation!" he heard Tonk screaming. But something died within Charley, and he realized it was no use screaming. They were caught and caught for good.

The chopper hovered for a minute or two and then landed ten yards away. David Many Hearts and Swami jumped out. Swami carried a shotgun, while David Many Hearts worked furiously with some lines from the net. Their cries, their questions were ignored. Then they heard the chopper engine roar into life again. There were a few bumps, the gust of the chopper's rotor blades seemed directly above them, and they felt themselves lifting.

"Holy smoke! I don't believe this!" Charley yelled. He and Tonk rolled into each other like fish in a trawler's net. The ground pulled away. Charley was face down. An ineffable sadness flooded his heart as he watched each clod of dirt, every pebble and rock, every clump of sagebrush and living thing of the earth recede. This was worse than any pain, or even any fear of pain. This was the most unthinkable fear of all, fear of the end. This cannot be happening to me, was all he could think. Kids don't die this way. But then another voice said, Yes, yes they do. That other voice kept talking—you think it all happens in hospitals, kids with leukemia, kids with crazy tumors, kids with parents by their sides holding their hands. Well, this is the other way kids die—violent and alone, as victims of other humans. His eyes stretched open till they hurt in stunned disbelief at what was actually happening to him, at the cold realization that he had absolutely no control. And you thought you were afraid of rattlesnakes? The other voice chortled. Ha-ha-ha! The same thunking cadences of the choppers blades. The whole sky laughing at his stupidity!

David Many Hearts pushed the floor stick between his legs, and the chopper moved forward now toward a ridge of broken red hills. As they drew closer the hills loomed larger and from Charley's view appeared like a red rock maze cut with deep, narrow canyons. He dared not even look over at Tonk, whose body was squashed up next to him. There was a change in the sound of the engines.

Charley craned his neck. The sun flashed on a bright patch of metal on one side of the underbelly of the chopper. Then the tail rotor blades began to angle differently. The chopper was turning to the left. There was another change in the staccato rhythm and Charley noticed they were going down. He must have changed the angle of the main set of rotors. He looked down again. Holy shit! Needles of red rock seemed inches from his stomach. They were hovering over one section of the ridge. It seemed endless. Then they felt a forward surge and they moved off a bit, but not up. If Charley had stuck his hand out he could have almost touched the top of some of the rock. They were looking for something, but what? Suddenly he saw it. They were hovering over a spire at the edge of a narrow box canyon, but when Charley looked directly down he saw nothing but a narrow dark void, a shaft cleft into the rock. "Oh no!' He gasped with terror at what he knew was to be his coffin.

# 32

"You sure you can do this?" Swami looked over at David Many Hearts nervously, as David maneuvered the Sikorsky S-76 over the opening in the rocks.

"Piece of cake. Try doing this in a monsoon with enemy fire." He was thinking about Con Thien and dropping netloads of ammo, rations, and medical supplies choppered in from Dong Ha. They would fly barely above the ground to evade detection from observers north of the DMZ, but once they got there the terrain was chinked with well-camouflaged caves full of North Vietnamese artillerymen who had them boresighted with 152-mm. guns.

"Let out on that rope a little."

Swami Ben-ji released a lever and another seven feet paid out, from which the net bag was suspended. "That enough?"

"Yeah, looks fine. Got 'em in there now."

It was a slow extinguishing of light. First there were the thin gray shadows accumulating above and all around them, and then, as Charley felt the net lower, the sky above shrank smaller and the darkness pressed in. And then there was the drop.

# 33

This time the Guardians of the Petal Way were not called. It was believed that Pahata had already left, but she hadn't wanted to go until she was sure of the mission's success, despite Swami's and David Many Hearts's urging. So she had secluded herself for the rest of the morning and after they returned she had been sneaked out a back exit, veiled in saffron robes, not her customary white.

The chopper had just landed. The rotors continued going as she boarded.

"Mission accomplished," Swami said firmly, then added, "David did a superb job."

"I wonder when they'll come." Pahata looked directly at Swami.

"They are not going to come for a long time. It's only eleven-thirty in the morning. He is not going to be discovered missing until this evening. We will be long gone. The people in Utah think you have already arrived, by the way, and that you cannot see them immediately because of a private channeling."

"What did you do?"

"Surneesh flew in the other chopper. They think you're in it. Just flew over enough to establish your presence, then scooted off."

"Surneesh is great. He never asks questions."

"You're not kidding," David Many Hearts said. "We even propped up a dummy of you in the seat next to him, just in case anybody from the ground looked closely for two people. Never said a word."

"We're set," Swami said confidently, "and in twenty minutes you are going to be sitting down with the C.E.O of Great Western Thermal Clean Fuels."

"How much did you say they want us to invest?"

"They're looking for five, six million." Swami paused. "I think it might be worth it. The PR value alone of your being associated with such an environmentally responsible outfit, and one that provides cheap fuel, could be terrific. You could really play this into something, Harriet. I was thinking about it last night. You know, young Joe Kennedy did that whole fuel-for-the-poor thing back in Boston. It made him very credible as a congressional candidate. He was no longer just the cut-up kid with the political silver spoon in his mouth."

"Yeah, well, let's not jump too far ahead. One thing at a time, one day at a time."

She settled back in her seat. David pressed on the rotor-blade pedals and the chopper headed due north toward the Grand Canyon and the Arizona-Utah border.

# 34

Archie and Calista were driving back from Phoenix. The grade of the highway seemed to have imperceptibly increased and with the flat expanse ahead Calista imagined that she could almost see the curve of the earth. Through a combination of light and limpid air the earth seemed to have attained a geometric clarity. Sunset was just degrees away and the horizon appeared like a soft opalescent border. As the sun sank the moon hovered high above the horizon like an immense translucent pearl. Equidistant between the moonrise and the sunset a red hill erupted from the desert bathed in the dying light of the day. Calista wished that she had brought her watercolors. But even just to stop for a few minutes and drink it in was exhilarating. She could never explain what it was that touched her so deeply about that red hill.

They had both gotten out and leaned against the hood of the truck for a few minutes in silence.

It was their Hopi break, as Calista had come to think of it. Almost every day at this time she and Archie found time to stand and watch the sun go down. Archie had told her about how the Hopi believed that their villages had grown from the ground like trees and that their houses had deep roots. They fed the roots, the health of the house, and the village by work and ritual. And at the end of the day, as they stood in their doorways the rays of the sun would wash away their weariness. Calista liked the notion especially that one's purpose, after all the hard work, was to enjoy the beauty of the day.

Three hours later Calista was hating herself for loving the sunset.

"He would never just go off like this. I know Charley. He would leave a note or something."

"No note," Brian said.

"None that I could find," Ted Moran echoed. The crew stood around with tense expressions. They were perplexed when they had returned and not found Charley in camp. They had begun to worry around dinnertime, especially since it was Charley's night to help Steve in the kitchen and he was very responsible about showing up for chores of this sort.

"Did anybody check to see if anything is missing from Charley's tent that would suggest where he might have gone?"

"Let me do that. I know his stuff and his mess," Calista said, swallowing a sob.

She was back within five minutes. "Both his canteens are gone and his backpack and I think a sweatshirt. I'm pretty sure he had brought an MIT sweatshirt."

"Okay," Archie said quickly. "I think I have a pretty good idea of where he might have gone."

"You do!"

Calista felt something within her soar. Every molecule of her being depended on Charley's existence. Life was worth nothing to her. . . . She did not complete the thought. All those stories about lost children came back to her, the children on the milk cartons. She even somehow knew the phrases that accompanied these terrible scenarios of missing children. The patient cops counseling the parents not to give up hope but gently preparing them for the worst of eventualities, explaining that with each passing hour the chances become slimmer of finding a child.

She felt the minutes oozing out of the day drop by drop, like blood. She was being slowly bled to death. There would be a time when she would look back on these first hours as a time of great hope, a time of chances and then she would torture herself even further by remembering how she had stood by the road with Archie and loved a goddam sunset. She hated it all now; the earth, the sun, this goddam land that had killed her husband and now might have taken her son.

# 35

I'm too young to die, thought Charley, and he's too old to be killed. It made no sense whatsoever. But then again, it did. Anyone who had lasted as long as Tonk deserved death at the hands of something better than David Many Hearts and Fat Ass. The fear was gone now. The anger made it go away and Charley felt something cold and hard coalesce inside him. He was going to get them out of here, and it would not be the last thing he did. Water wasn't a problem, as it was so dark they weren't perspiring and Charley still had the canteens with him. They were still in the net just as when they had been dropped into the shaft minutes before.

Luckily when the chopper dropped them it had not been a long drop at all, just a few feet, and the impact was soft, for the bottom of this shaft was sandy. However, they were fairly tangled up in the net. Tonk was on top of him and had begun squirming.

"You okay, Tonk?"

"Yeah, you're not the greatest cushion. What'd you say your name was again?"

"Charley."

"Well, Charley, let me tell you something. I'm tough. I don't break easy 'cause I can bend." He had rolled off Charley and the two were now trying to sort out their arms and legs from the net. "I'm like an aspen or a lodgepole pine. Lot of sap in me. So it ain't gonna be my bones that goes, and it ain't gonna be my ticker neither, though I got a touch of the high blood pressure." They had now maneuvered themselves into upright sitting positions next to each other. Their eyes had become accustomed to the darkness and they could see each other.

"So, what's it going to be?" Charley asked, turning to Tonk.

"My brain?" Tonk said matter-of-factly.

"Your brain?" Charley whispered.

"Yep, sorry 'bout that."

"Well, how come?"

"I just can't remember like I use to and I get these seizures. They call it M.I.A."

"M.I.A.?"

"No, no wait a minute. Not M.I.A. That's Missing in Action. See, what'd I tell you?—I forgit. But that's not bad, M.I.A., 'cause that's what happens to my brain—gets kind of missing in action. I take these pills for it, but I don't have them with me. . . ."

"Let me ask you something," Charley said.

"Shoot."

"Before that helicopter plucked us up you were telling me about why you were out here . . . something about Claudia Perkins and parcels of land on the old water system."

"Yes, by gum!" Tonk's eyes burned fiercely in the dim light. "It's that woman of theirs, that Goddy lady."

"What about her?"

"Smart of you, Charley, to ask me this now, while I'm clear. That little chopper ride kind of blew the cobwebs out."

"Okay, what about Pahata Ra."

"Why, darn it, it came to me the other day. I was going over some water company stuff. The new company, the one Claudie and I started back in the forties, or maybe it was the thirties. I don't know."

"You and Claudie have a water company?"

"Her grubstake. She put up most of the money. I kicked in as much as I could. See, the whole town used to work off the old Palatki system. A rancher came in here years ago, oh, back in the 1890s and put in the old one. I s'pose it was good for them times, but the water tasted lousy, plentiful but lousy. So Claudia got sick of drinking water that looked like pig swill. There are private water companies all over Arizona. She just started her own. Got more modern filtering technology and all that. Only problem was, it was sparse. Not much flow and in bad seasons we were dependent on the old system to feed in. The original idea was to use the old Palatki just for irrigation, but in dry times we were still dependent on it. Course, with the new filtering down in town we could clean it up pretty good, by the time it got there. Claudie had the rights to let it feed in 'cause she owned several parcels of land on the old system. The old system fell out of the jurisdiction of the water commission 'cause even though a company is privately owned it has to answer to the commission." He paused. "Unless . . .

"Unless it's as old as the Palatki one, which is kind of grand-fathered in and doesn't have to answer to the commission in the same way as newer private systems. You see, you get so many hours each day during dry times for nonirrigational use from surface systems. . . ." Tonk had begun to spin off into a rambling discussion of compliance laws, statutes, and a variety of regula-tions covering Arizona's water use. He seemed lost in a morass of explanations about watersheds, public domain lands, some-thing called the Tri County Water Pact. He was just getting into the gallons per capita, for both humans, and cattle and sheep, and the Taylor Grazing Act of 1934 when Charley interrupted.

"But what about this Pahata and Claudia's parcels?"

"Oh yes! That she-devil. Well," Tonk continued, "I figured it out when I was sitting in my office one day. You know I'm the mayor of Red Forks. Have been since 1933, year before the grazing law passed and just when Mr. Roosevelt . . ."

Charley interrupted again. "Yes, you were sitting in your office and what did you figure out about Claudia and the parcels of land?" Steering Tonk back to the subject reminded Charley of going through the supermarket with his mom when they got a cart with a bum wheel. You had to keep on it to make it go straight down an aisle.

"Well, I took out that water-ordinance map and then I got out the record of property sales for the past three years. A lot had turned over, little pieces, the kind people forget about maybe. You know, like Annie Fuentes herself—she's the sheriff. She was elected after old Pokey, Polk Fitzwater, died. Coy was acting sheriff for a while but then . . ."

"Yes," said Charley, "Annie Fuentes."

"Oh yes, as I was saying . . . what was I saying?"

Oh no, thought Charley. Talking with Tonk was like going through a maze, hit a wall. Back up. Retrace steps. Do I turn left or right here? Keep the image in mind. "Annie Fuentes and something about a lot of property changing hands."

"Oh yes. She sold that little piece just opposite the old Red Forks Hotel, but on the back side. Sold it to help a nephew of hers go to veterinary school. Nobody thought much about it at the time. Some guy from the East bought it. All through his lawyers. You know the old asthma story. We do have the greatest number of asthmatics in the country here in Arizona. Matter of fact, some famous doctor once came through Red Forks doing a study. We all got to go down to Winslow and get free chest X rays."

"So she sold this land to an asthmatic from the East."

"Well, I think that was the story. I think he was an asthmatic. But then another one showed up."

"Another asthmatic?"

"No, just another person—forget his name—and he bought a parcel out the west end of town. It's not a very good parcel at all. Faces north and east; hardly no sun shines there at all. Kind of always like being in a hole."

"Yeah?"

"So now we're two down and that's not counting the stuff that Pahata is buying outright."

"What do you mean 'outright'?"

"Well, you see, I would've never used that term until I started thinking. You know that's the wonderful thing about thinking . . . these ideas."

" 'Outright,' Tonk, what do you mean?"

"You see, that she-devil had already bought the ranch and we all knew who bought it. She didn't try to hide anything. Then Claudia came and said that the guy who had bought the piece behind the old Red Forks Hotel had called her and asked about two of her parcels. I didn't think anything of it at the time, but then, I don't know, when she went away for that long time . . ." His eyes grew soft. He swallowed. "Oh, Lordy, that's why I'm out here! I'm looking for my Claudie." In the thin gray darkness Charley saw a tear begin to roll down the old face, across the fine patchworks of crisscrosses and wrinkles beneath his eyes, finding its way into the deep corrugations that creased his cheeks.

"Don't cry, Tonk." A desperation seized Charley. Tonk forgetting, getting confused was one thing, but Tonk crying was another. If they were ever going to get out of here they had to keep their wits even if some of them were a bit frayed around the edges.

"But something's happened to her. I know it, I just know. She ain't gone to Yuma. Sulena died years ago. Besides, she didn't much care for Sulena and she hated Yuma." Tonk paused. "Goddammit, they probably dropped her in one of these holes too!"

Charley had a feeling that Tonk might be right. But they were going to get out of this hole.

"Did they drop her in because of those land parcels?"

"Sure! See, that's the point. She owned the last three parcels on the system. They get those and they control the works—the Palatki and the new system as well, since it was so dependent on the old one. And what have we been having out here for the last three years but a drought. Worst one in thirty years. They get those parcels they can dry us all out. They can turn the faucet on and off whenever they want."

It all made sense now. Charley remembered standing in the lobby of the main building with the architectural master plan drawings and the models. He remembered his mom asking about the structures that turned out to house the water filtration systems. They wanted it all—land, water, people, and they were ready to kill for it. Tonk had begun mumbling about Claudie again. What the heck was he going to do to get them out of here? Was there any hope with a ninety-year-old man who was definitely on the ragged edge?

"Tonk!" He nearly barked the name. "Quit crying. We've got

to get out of here. They don't have Claudie's land and they might not have Claudie. We've got to get out of here. You're the mayor of Red Forks. You've got to do something about it!"

Tonk looked up. "You're right." He paused. "So what are we going to do?"

"Well, I have to think and I can't think when you're crying."

"Oh well, then I'll be quiet," Tonk said, suddenly contrite, rather like a small child who has been reprimanded. He looked up at Charley inquisitively. "You thinking?"

"Trying to."

"You know, thinking is a wonderful thing . . . because . . ." His voice began rambling off in the darkness, thin and scratchy, like a skein of yarn Charley imagined tossed about by a kitten, loosening, unrolling, unraveling. But he'd rather have Tonk like this than crying, that was for sure.

**36**———————————Agnes Bessie stood in her kitchen looking out the window over the sink. She was snipping back her catnip and pinching dead leaves off the geranium plants on the sill. But she wasn't paying much attention to the plants, for outside Andrea Kaye was leading a gentleman around and pointing at various details of the old adobe jail. The man was an architect. Agnes knew it, although no one had told her so. She could just tell, and every now and then she caught a word or fragment of a phrase about foundations or roof beams.

There was no other reason why Andrea would be sashaying around the jail with this feller in tow. He wasn't a Pahattie either. Probably came over from Winslow, or maybe even Phoenix. And, Lord have mercy, she never had seen anyone dressed like Andrea, especially for a business meeting. She was wearing the skimpiest, clingiest little shorts. Her *chiblets*, as Bert used to call them, were pooching out the back and on one she could clearly see a rainbow tattoo. Agnes had good eyes. Only needed her glasses for close work. The architect had good eyes too. He was more interested in Andrea's *chiblets* than the jail. And he wasn't passing up those jiggling boobies either. It seemed to be against these folks' religion to wear brassieres. They did not believe in foundation garments. Agnes Bessie did. Although she was thin, she always wore a panty girdle and a brassiere with either stays or wire inserts. God gave women a little extra flesh here and there and it all added up to a lovely form. It wasn't right to go about letting it flap around; not only was it unseemly, but it broke down the tissue and then you really wound up a mess. Agnes's eyes narrowed. "Sweet pea," she whispered, "in another sixty years you're going to look like hell."

Of course, whom did she herself have to look good for? Bert had been dead for twenty years, but they'd done it right up to the end, just about. And who knew if it were true about Claudie and Tonk, but why not? He'd go up there couple times a month and spend the night. There was plenty you could do even if you couldn't quite do it all the way.

The geraniums suddenly were a coral blur as Agnes remembered a time toward the end with Bert. Of course they didn't know then that he had cancer. It came on so sudden. Oh but dear, she hated to think about these things and now poor Tonk gone too, and Lord knew what happened to Claudie—not a living relative down there in Yuma. Claudie never mentioned anything about Sulena dying, but then, they never did get on. Not many of them left now, a ragtag few. How could they stand up to these new folks with their weird ideas? Didn't these folks have any sense of what home was? What it meant? She watched as Andrea and the architect reappeared from around the corner of the jail. Oh well, no sense getting all weepy now. She gave a little sniff and straightened her shoulders. The architect's back was turned to Andrea now and she was tracing some sort of outline on his back. Most likely something to do with one of her nutty crystal medicine cures. She'd probably be sticking rocks all over him. If people would only wear good foundation garments they wouldn't have to go in for this harebrained stuff. That reminded her of an arrowhead she'd found the other day just outside town when she was taking her evening walk. It was in with her collection. Right in the kitchen drawer. She pulled open the drawer.

There were at least thirty points, the archaeologist's name for arrowheads, all neatly lined up on cotton batting. She took her new one out. It was delicate, with serrated edges. It looked as if it came out of the Clovis point tradition and it was made out of a real pretty pinky-gray quartz with a nice milk-white vein down the center. She turned it over in her hand, and thought about the maker of it. Whoever had knapped it had been real careful to keep that vein right in the middle. She had to remember to show it to Archie. Archie was so nice about that stuff. A lot of the archaeologists got all huffy if you found things and kept them for yourself. They seemed to think that if you weren't some scholar with a bunch of letters after your name you had no business picking the stuff up, let alone keeping it. But Archie wasn't that way. He knew that Agnes was keeping all the things for the Red Forks museum. He believed in the museum. He believed in the people of Red Forks. She was ashamed of having just called them a ragtag few, even if it was just in her thoughts. Archie never thought of them that way. He talked to them and asked them questions and even quoted them in his scholarly articles and books. She looked at the point in her hand again and then glanced up at Andrea Kaye and the architect. They were standing real close to one another and giggling now. Dollars to doughnuts they'll be in the sack by tonight, Agnes thought, and closed her hand into a fist over the arrowhead.

# 37_____ "Thinking," Tonk was saying,
"is truly a wonderful thing."

"It sure is!" Charley said suddenly. Here he had been imagining Tonk's voice unrolling like a ball of yarn in the darkness, and, my gosh! Duh! How dumb can you be? They were sitting right on their own tangled pile of yarn and it was the very means of their escape. Boy, had Fat Ass and David Many Hearts blown it when they left the net behind. Dickhead!

"You got a knife on you, Tonk?"

"Yep. You need it?"

"Yeah. I need seven or eight, to tell you the truth."

"What you thinkin' of doin' . . . ?" Tonk paused. "What's your name again?"

"Charley."

"Charley, that's right."

"I'm thinking of doing that thing rock climbers do when they stick in pitons." Charley was standing up and surveying the shaft they were in. It was at least eighteen feet deep. The walls were red sandstone. That meant they'd crumble easily and probably couldn't support the weight of the net, let alone both of them climbing up it. If only there were some way that Charley could get up, then leverage the net for some mechanical advantage and haul up Tonk. He stooped over and picked up part of the net. It was heavy, darned heavy. Maybe as much as one hundred pounds.

"Here you go," said Tonk.

It was an impressive knife. No little Swiss Army knife full of convenient gadgets. It was a Bowie hunting knife. When Charley pulled it from the sheath, its blade shone brightly, all nine inches of it. The last three inches angled off thirty degrees, finishing in a tip. Good design sense—lessened the resistance and allowed more plunge with the least amount of effort per unit of surface area. The handle was bone and the hilt stainless steel. An all-business knife. It would hold all right. It could probably sustain the net, plus them, if positioned right. But he had to get it up there and high enough, high enough to help them out of the hole, and he did not want to leave it behind. What he needed really were two knives like this. With two such knives he could have two steps that he could keep moving up the wall by alternating hand- and footholds. There was one problem, however, even with that, which was that he could climb right out, but not Tonk. But then he could carry the net with him and secure it above so Tonk could climb out. He liked this idea. He had to think about it a bit more. He eyed Tonk and wondered how good a climber he would be. Climbing a big heavy net like this wouldn't be too difficult. Plenty of good purchases available. But then again, it was straight up, and Tonk was almost ninety. He had, however, survived the airlift and drop.

"Whatcha lookin' at?" Tonk asked.

"You."

"Me?" Tonk laughed. "Handsome devil, aren't I?"

"How good a climber are you?"

"I can still climb on a horse. One knee got a little arthritis. But the arthritis gives me more trouble in my hands than anyplace else."

"Yeah?"

"Yeah? You see." He held out his hands. They were gnarled and bumpy with enormous veins and swollen finger joints. "Can't close them." He held his hands palm up and Charley saw him trying to curl his fingers into a fist. But they froze. Not much good for getting a purchase on a vertical plane, Charley thought. But he didn't want to let go of this idea.

What if the plane were not so vertical, more of a slope than a sheer angle? Then Tonk could crawl up it. He could get more purchase from his feet and even his knees. Same principle as a rear-wheel-drive automobile. He wouldn't have to pull with his hands, just use them as a steadying force. All the exertion would come from behind. But how to make a slope out of the net?

He was confident now that he could climb out without the net. Between the Bowie knife and the Swiss Army knife he knew he could haul himself out. It was just Tonk. He got up and paced around the small space that was no more than eight by eight feet.

"Expectin' a baby? Hee-hee," laughed Tonk. This young feller tickled him. "Never had any children myself, least none that I know'd about. Used to go over to the cathouses when I was riding up in Montana. Them whores were real nice up in Montana. Felt real good after winter branding to snuggle down, but I never put my brand on any kid. Don't think so. As I was sayin' about brandin', now that's when this hand arthritis began to act up. I could wrap my fingers round the branding iron and did I ever tell you, Hank . . ." Tonk was spinning off again into an imbroglio of memories that went back seventy-five years to when he cowpunched in Montana. He kept calling Charley Hank and there was someone named Doris who had the biggest titties this side of the divide.

"Okay," Charley said slowly, "I think I've got it. He stood holding a U shank and bolt. The net had terminated in an eye loop and the U shank and bolt had obviously been used to lace a longer rope through by which the net was suspended from the chopper. When they had let them down into this hole they had merely untied the rope and pulled it through the shank back into the chopper. The shank remained attached to the net through the eye loop. The bolt was six inches long perhaps. If Charley could jam it into the farthest corner of the shaft he could get a forty-five-degree-angle slope as opposed to a ninety-degree angle for the net. Thirty or twenty-five would have been preferable, but this was going to have to do for Tonk. Now to run a few tests to get himself out. Charley doubted he weighed much more than the net. Last time he had weighed himself he was just over one hundred. Could a Swiss Army knife support one hundred pounds just temporarily while he moved the Bowie knife? Wait a minute. It wouldn't have to support his entire weight if he could distribute it over another base, like a shallow step. Wasn't that what rock climbers did? Every little crack or protrusion in the rock became a step in a staircase.

**38**————————————Later, Pahata Ra and Swami
Ben-ji with David Many Hearts at the controls were flying back.
Pahata was nervous.

"I think we're going to be okay, Pahata," Swami was saying.
"I think you're overreacting. We've got our alibi. There are pictures of you in the Utah papers."

"Yeah, and we told you, Pahata, there is no way they are going
to find them, any trace of them. First of all, they aren't anywhere
near the area and even if they were, you just don't find two people
who've been dropped into a place like this."

"You say it's out by the Needles?" she asked.

"Yeah, you want to fly over it?"

"Yes," she said somberly.

This was always the way it was with Harriet, Swami thought.
She could work herself into a lather in no time. Sometimes
Valium helped if they could get her to take it early on, but the
jitters had set in. Only way to quell them was to show her the
place now.

**39**————————————If it hadn't been for the crack
that had started about eight and a half feet up, Charley did not
know if it would have been nearly as easy. He had been able to
wedge a hand in that crack and a good part of one foot. With
his free hand he yanked the rope attached to the Bowie knife as
a retrieval system. He had taken a four-foot length from the net
for this purpose. He had tied to his belt another twenty-foot length
extricated from the net. The other end of this longer rope was

still part of the webbing of the net. He planned to haul the net up this way. And perhaps if he could gain something, that would give him enough mechanical advantage that he could haul Tonk up on the net so he wouldn't have to do too much climbing.

"Nearly there, Tonk. Another four feet. That'll do it."

"Okay, Hank. Who you got ridin' drag?" Tonk was lost in a welter of cattle-driving memories.

"No, Tonk," Charley said patiently in a soft voice as he took a rest with his feet braced against one wall at an angle and his armpit slung over the handle of the Bowie knife. "I am not Hank. I am Charley, and we're getting ourselves out of a hole. This is not a cattle drive. You remember Claudie, don't you?"

"Oh yes!" The voice seemed to clench.

"Okay, I'm sorry, but I've got to keep you on the track."

"I know, I know," Tonk sighed from fifteen feet below him. "I'm just like one of those little stray dogies." He was off again.

In another fifteen minutes Charley was out. He felt as if he were on top of the world, and not ten feet away was a formation of red rock made to order. He flopped the net on top of it, walked back to the edge of the shaft, and called down, "Okay, Tonk, you ready to get out of that hole?"

"Yes siree!"

# 40 ————————David had reduced the pitch

of the rotors and they were skimming over the points of the spires that combed this wide ridge as densely as the bristles of a brush. "It's right in here somewhere," David was saying. The ridge itself dipped slightly, forming a kind of saddleback. "Okay we're getting close."

They were hovering now not more than ten or fifteen feet above the ground. "Holy shit!" David suddenly said.

"What is it?" Pahata barked.

"Oh my God." Swami was just now seeing what David had already spotted.

"It's the fucking net!"

"What net?" asked Pahata, confused.

"The net we dropped them in. They fucking got out."

"Oh, great! Great!" Pahata exploded. "What a pair of assholes I've got here." She curled her hands into two small fists and began beating on Swami's shoulders. Her fists seemed to bounce right off.

"Shut up!" roared David. "You want me to crash?" That seemed to be a sobering thought for Pahata.

"What are we going to do?" she began wailing.

"We're going to hunt for them," said David.

"David's right, Harriet."

"No use losing your cool now. Just stay calm."

"I just don't understand this." Pahata began whimpering. "This twerp, this twerpy kid, he's going to ruin everything." She slammed her fists against her knees. "I could never stand his mother and now him. They're going to ruin it all!" She stomped a sandaled foot on the rubber mat of the chopper's floor.

"We will find them," David Many Hearts said grimly.

Charley and Tonk had taken refuge under a rock shelf overhang as soon as they heard the thrumping. The chopper was flying very low, going over the terrain like a fine-toothed comb. A blast of hot air and dust flattened them against the overhang's wall, and the chopper hovered not fifty feet away. Charley curled himself into the tightest ball he could. He had prayed that Tonk, who seemed to be fading in and out of reality and the present time frame, would just keep his wits about him for enough consecutive lucid minutes to try and figure out where they were. But he couldn't even think of that now. The gusts were slamming into them at gale force. He peeked from a small chink of space under the bend of his elbow that was shielding his face. God, they were close! His heart nearly stopped. He could see Pahata's white robes in the passenger seat, the blank, shimmering, iridescent eyes.

Then the gusts lessened. The chopper turned and climbed.

"They'll be back," Tonk muttered as they both unfolded themselves and came out from under the rock overhang. The chopper floated off. They watched it disappear over the ridge and become a small speck as harmless as a gnat. The sky seemed to swallow it. But the air for some time was still seized by the thrumping staccato of the chopper like an ominous promise of its return.

## 41

Calista was thinking about Peter Pan, that last rough sketch she had made before leaving Cambridge, of Peter standing on a rock looking out across the stretch of sea, his chest thrust out, his chin bravely tilted, the drum beating within his chest, beating the tattoo—"To die will be an awfully big adventure." She buried her face in her hands and hunched forward on the sleeping bag in her tent. Archie had set off with Brian, Ted, and Steve to search the area where he and Charley had been two days before, where they had discovered the tracks. Archie had first gone to the area the evening before, but the light had petered out before the tracks and they'd had to give up. But they had returned before dawn this morning to resume the search. With each passing hour Calista felt something leaden growing within her. It was as if her whole being were turning to lead. This was no good. She had to will herself to think positively. Was there any way that a mother could somehow telepathically communicate with a child? Could these genetic bonds have some kind of telepathic dimension? He was clever, now could she will him courage?

. . .

Archie Baldwin rose from his knees. Why did everything, all the juniper and piñon, all the low-growing desert scrub, look so squashed and broken right here, at this point where the tracks ended? He had found Charley's tracks and Tonk's. They had ended abruptly about two thousand feet up from where they had first started.

"Hey, I've got some orange peel here!" Ted Moran called out from a few feet away.

"Guess what I've got." Steve Child said in even tones.

"What's that?" Archie looked sharply to where Steve was standing.

"I've got some kind of large tread marks."

"Up here?" Archie was immediately beside Steve.

"An A.T.V.?" Brian asked.

"No," said Archie grimly, "a helicopter." He paused. "It's time for some law enforcement."

# 42

"Well, where are we?" Charley said, coming out of the rock shelter.

"God's country," Tonk answered. "Any sign of those strays, Hank?"

"Oh, rats!" muttered Charley. This was like a maze within a maze. There was the maze of the canyon-latticed land and then there was the one of Tonk's mind. They were going to have to find their way through both if they were to survive.

"Tonk," Charley began in a tired but steady voice, "I'm Charley, you're Tonk. This is Arizona and we're lost."

"We're not lost, young fellow. How often do I have to tell you? Just confused. I know who I am. You know who you are. Where'd you say we were?"

"Arizona."

"See, that's a start."

"Okay, but where? Remember they flew us here in a helicopter."

"Well, we're somewhere on the Colorado Plateau."

Charley bit his lip. The Colorado Plateau was a block of earth that comprised the top third of the state of Arizona, extending northward into Utah, east and northeast into New Mexico and Colorado, and west to Charley did not know where.

"Could you be a little more specific, Tonk?" He made a point of always addressing Tonk now by his name, as there was always the threat of his becoming unhinged entirely and forgetting everything. He had not so far done that. Ever since Charley had told him who he was Tonk had kept that in mind. It was just the time and place references that seemed to slide about for Tonk, and Charley's identity. "Remember when I first met you I was coming up that trail, that one off the Old Palatki Wash Road? And then that helicopter scooped us up and brought us here? It was about a five- to eight-minute trip. No more. Does that help you at all?"

"Yeah, it might." Tonk paused. "Do you know which direction we were flying."

Charley sighed. That would be hard to tell. It was afternoon when the chopper had picked them up. And dangling from a net under the belly of a helicopter was a disorienting experience to say the least. He closed his eyes and tried to remember if he had noticed the sun's position. But the net had turned slowly and all he could recall was sometimes the sun striking one part of his body and then another. If only he could place things in any kind of configuration. He really just remembered looking down for the most part, watching that ridge combined with spires pass beneath them. It had seemed so bizarre at the time it would forever be couched in feelings of unreality. It had been like being in one of the Omnimax movies that he went to at the Boston Museum of Science. The only thing missing had been the dramatic music. But then he did remember something, a shadow.

No, not a shadow at all! Quite the opposite—a bright glinting thing, an oval patch on one side of the underside of the chopper. Then when the chopper had begun to hover and turn the patch became readable—Sikorsky S-76. So what did that mean? It meant that they had been flying on a course so that the sun was shining on that patch and when they turned they must have turned away from the sun. Charley closed his eyes and concentrated. Which side had the the patch been on? That was the only way he would ever be able to figure out if they had been flying north or south. East and west were eliminated because they had not been flying directly into the sun or away from it. It was hitting them laterally. But which lateral? This was like trying to do the orienting the hatchets problem on the IQ test while standing on your head spinning. The patch was on the left side of the chopper! It came to him in a flash. The image burned brightly in his eye. He could place it in relation to the skids and their struts. So if the sun was illuminating the patch from the left it meant that they had to be flying north.

"Come here, Tonk." Charley crouched down and took out his Swiss Army knife and opened a blade. He made an X in the dirt. "If this X is Red Forks, where is the Old Palatki Wash Road in relation to it? South?"

Tonk squatted down. A gnarled finger extended and scratched lightly at the dirt. "Here and a little east," he said.

"Yeah." Charley nodded. "It's south of Red Forks and a little east."

"So what you figuring, Charley?"

Charley's heart skipped a beat. He had actually called him by his right name and not Hank. Maybe if he could keep things concrete enough, Tonk's brains would not entirely slip their mounts. He'd better make hay while these neurotransmitters were shining. "Okay," Charley continued, "I've pretty much figured out that from the trail off the Old Palatki Wash Road we flew north. Can you figure out . . ." He didn't finish the sentence. Tonk stood up and surveyed the land.

"By gum! We're on the Defiance Rim!"

"Great!' Charley leapt up and nearly screamed. "Which way's home?"

"Not far at all—fifty, seventy-five miles to downtown Red Forks."

"Fifty or seventy-five miles? Tonk, we'll never make it."

"Nonsense, boy, why once back in the blizzard of thirty-eight, I'd gone back up to Montana that winter to help on the old Stapleton Ranch and we got caught out. Remember that, Hank . . . ?"

# 43

      As posses went, it was not a prepossessing sight. Not like the one that had gone after Butch Cassidy and the Sundance Kid, Calista was thinking. Calista and Archie were in Annie Fuentes's office. Annie had just sworn in Coy, Lucille Greyeyes, Agnes, assorted other town council members, and the entire archaeology team as deputies. They were all authorized now to carry weapons and make arrests under Article 2, part B of the town's civil defense code. Archie was on the phone trying to get hold of the district attorney in Phoenix, but he was not in. He was at a Kiwanis Club luncheon honoring the mayor. The assistant D.A. was over in Flagstaff. When Archie tried the Best Western, where the luncheon was being held he couldn't get through on the phone. There was some sort of problem and he kept getting reservations. Then they offered to give him an 800 number.

"Archie." Annie Fuentes looked over. "Come on. We'll just go over there ourselves. I have all the warrants in order. We can't arrest them on this evidence anyhow. D.A.'s not going to be able to either. All we can do is bring them in for questioning at this point. And technically you can't even file a missing persons report on Charley yet. Seventy-two hours have to elapse before you can do that."

"Okay," Archie said, and put down the phone. Annie Fuentes was incredibly organized. She would probably handle this thing more efficiently than anyone from the district attorney's office. She had raised five kids, two of her own and three of a widowed alcoholic sister's, had managed to get them all through high school, some through junior colleges, and some through Arizona State. She herself had gone back to school and become an LPN. Her own husband had up and left years before. She'd do okay.

"Just excuse me a minute," Annie said. "Be right back." She went through a door into a back room. What nobody knew about Annie was that in addition to being homemaker, LPN, community organizer, and sheriff, she was an avid reader of crime stories. She belonged to organizations with funny names like the Nero Wolfes and Sisters in Crime and the Mystery Writers of America. These were organizations for both fans and authors of mysteries. She opened up a file drawer and took out a recent newsletter from one of these organizations that had a short piece on interrogation techniques. It was an excerpt from a book by Rudolph Caputo, who had had extensive experience in the fine art of interrogation for both police and intelligence operations. She skimmed the article again. Caputo's three principles were written in boldface.

1. **We were born to tell the truth** (she wasn't sure if that really could apply to Pahata Ra, but she had better go in thinking positive).

2. **Man is a talking animal**.

3. **We live in a world of persuasion**. There was a quote from the famous criminologist. "It is psychologically cruel to expect a suspect to admit a crime immediately. We must pave the way." In other words, persuade the person to tell the truth in the same way we are persuaded through television and radio to eat, drink, and think.

That's exactly what she was going to do—pave the way.

· · ·

Annie Fuentes had been waiting her entire two terms for a crime. It looked as if she might have one now.

# 44

There had been nothing left to do except to start walking. Charley was sure that between where they were and Red Forks they had to encounter a road, a car, a ranch, a hogan, or some sign of life. What Tonk Cullen had neglected to tell Charley was that although they were fifty or seventy-five miles from Red Forks they were less than fifteen miles from the far northwest corner of Rancho Radiance.

For the most part they had confined their walking to the cool part of the day. There was no sense killing themselves slowly in the sun. And it probably wouldn't have been that slowly for Tonk. For the last half day he had been more out of reality than in it. Though he never complained, Charley felt that in the last three quarters of an hour his breathing had sounded slightly irregular. The sun was sinking fast and this would be their best traveling time. They shouldn't waste it, but on the other hand they had to conserve Tonk's energy because sometimes they had to move and think very fast, especially when the helicopter came back. And it had been back twice now. But Tonk had been excellent on these occasions. Wherever his mind had wandered to—an old trail drive in Montana, a cathouse in Casper—he snapped right back. He had an instinct for the danger that was at hand. The danger in some ways might remain slightly abstract and unnameable. For example, he knew that the helicopter meant trouble but was becoming very hazy about Pahata, the scheme to buy up real estate, and his own efforts to track down the parcels on the old water system. He even seemed to be forgetting Claudie. But his instincts for survival were nonetheless keen.

"Don't you move a goddam inch!" he barked.

Charley was about to ask why when he realized why: a fat rattlesnake was sleeping in the last shadow of the day cast by the lip of a rock that Charley had been heading to sit down on. He stopped dead in his tracks. He felt something drop inside him and his breath locked in his throat. Then he began shaking all over. He couldn't take his eyes off the snake. The precise geometric patterning of its skin, the diamond-shaped head tucked under a coil of the body. This was what had killed his father almost four years ago. This was their nemesis, their own personal family Satan, and yet he did not feel anger now—only fear. The whole landscape, the entire country welled up around him from the jagged red spires of the ridge to the gouged-out canyons with intimations of death. And here he was alone with a ninety-year-old man in the middle of nowhere, looking down on death's head. Was he a fool or what? There was no way they were going to get out of here. Maybe he should welcome this coil of death that slept in front of him.

"Whatcha doin' shittin' in your pants? Move, boy!" Tonk snarled at him. "Whatcha say yer name was?"

"Charley."

"Charley! Goddammit, I'm gettin' tired of kickin' ass round here. Now move it."

Charley took a step back and then walked around the snake still sleeping.

"That's it, boy . . . whatcha name again?"

"Charley."

"That's it, Charley, give the critter a wide berth. I think I see some organ pipe down there."

They had not been starving. Part and parcel of Tonk's survival instincts was a sure knowledge of edible plant life out here and where to find it. Charley didn't particularly care for the taste of any of it, but he was reluctant to use up their last orange. As he sat now nibbling very slowly on the red, plum-sized fruit of a organ pipe cactus he was thinking how proud his mother would be of him for "broadening his tastes." She was constantly after

him about the narrowness of his diet and how he was the only
kid in Cambridge who ate white bread. Well, here I am, Mom,
chowing down on some organ pipe cactus balls! How's that for
exotic eats?

"Get some of this, mesquite beans and saguaro fruit you got
yourself a feast. Papago Indians, that's all they eat. Saguaro and
mesquite. That's what Papago means—bean people. And we keep
moving on down like this we'll get into the saguaro country.
Plenty of juice, plenty of fruit. We can even build ourselves a
house out one of them things—Papagos do it all the time."

"One of what things?" Charley asked.

"Saguaro cactus—make great houses. Strong as oak."

Charley looked directly at Tonk. It suddenly occurred to him
that Tonk was in no rush to get back. He was perfectly happy
out here. The notion of hunkering down in a little saguaro hut
with a pile of mesquite beans was perfectly reasonable, maybe
even appealing, to Tonk. Hadn't Archie said that for an old geezer
like Tonk to die in the desert, in the country he loved, was not
such a bad end?

Was this the generation gap or what? The whole notion was
short on appeal for Charley. A little bachelor pad in the middle
of nowhere with Tonk! He didn't want to get overly mushy about
this kind of stuff but there were places he'd rather end his days
and things he would miss. His school had given a play just that
spring—*Our Town*. He remembered the part when Emily said
goodbye to all the things she would miss—clocks ticking, bread
baking . . . etc. etc. Some of those things on Emily's list were the
same things that he would have missed, too. Although at the time
he hadn't quite thought about it with the same keenness as now.

Somehow mesquite beans, saguaro huts, and rattlesnakes
didn't quite do it for Charley. What if he never saw his mom
again? Or Archie? And Matthew and Madame Morganstern, the
French teacher? He hated her, but she was good for so many
laughs. What was there to laugh at out here? It was pretty, no
doubt about it, but pretty wasn't funny. And what about his
computer and all his E-mail pals, those electronic friends that

he communicated with daily through the bulletin boards that netted all the computer freaks together? And what about girls? Amy? Oh God, poor Amy. Well, for the moment, she was probably better off than he was. He thought wistfully about Amy.

The first time he had ever seen her she was wearing a canary-yellow micro-miniskirt with a hot pink tank top and these outrageous painted sneakers. He loved the way she dressed. He liked girls who wore either all black or wild bright colors. If he had any criticism of Archie at all it was that his nieces and nephews were a tad preppy. They were all into Ralph Lauren. No vinyl, no leather. He didn't go for the totally punk look, not that gross-me-out punk style of the kids who hung around the out-of-town newsstand in Harvard Square, the ones with dyed mohawks and safety pins in their noses. That was definitely not to Charley's taste. But all that maroon and navy Archie's nieces wore! Too much. He thought that Amy made a nice "fashion statement." He had heard that expression from his mother. She actually had nothing but scorn for the idea of fashion statements.

An interviewer had once asked her if she was trying to make a fashion statement when she showed up at something in a tuxedo jacket. She had been furious. Books make statements, not clothes! Oh, how he missed his mother! Why did this have to happen? It was his fault. Tonk would have wandered in sooner or later. He looked over at Tonk now. He seemed totally lost in thought. He was away, far, far away, Charley was sure, off in Montana, in a blizzard, a cattle drive, his rheumy eyes distant with the unimaginable horizons.

# 45

But Tonk was not that far away really. No farther than the scent of the evening primrose that came on the edge of the wind blowing up from the canyon floor below. It made him think of Claudie. It was a true desert flower. There was a mess of them that grew in a swale behind her house, and she always had a bunch on the table and sometimes stuck one in her hair. She knew how to make a dusting powder from them. She learned that from the Indians. Oh, he remembered her—what, sixty, seventy years ago—sitting in the tin-lined copper tub, clouds of steam coming up all around her and a bright yellow blossom tucked behind her ear. Her face all shiny and pink, her eyes as bright and cloudless as the sky, her skin tawny as sun on the desert sand. And when she grew old and her skin began to wrinkle it was so fine that the wrinkles didn't even look bad, just like fine crackling on an old glazed jug. Had every tooth in her head, wits to spare, and could be frisky as a colt when she was in the mood. For more than sixty years they had understood each other perfectly. That was the whole point: two born loners who knew how to be together when they were alone, and alone when they were together. No overlaps, no mix-ups. They could go to bed together, do business together. For over forty years they'd run the best damn water company around. The most wonderful thing about Claudie, though, was her smile. It was not a ready smile. She was real spare with it. Not that she was a sourpuss. It was just slow to break, that smile, and when it did it wasn't one of those big, toothy bright ones. No, it was more quiet and clear like an evening star low on the horizon and just for you. And just like a star you might see on a very clear night you would think just maybe you could touch it, but you couldn't. She warn't no star, though.

"What's that, Tonk?"

"I said she warn't no star. She's a desert rose."

# 46_____Annie Fuentes was worrying

over how exactly to Mirandize Pahata Ra. She didn't want to just step right up to her and read her the law—the way they did it on television. This would not jibe with the gentle approach she had decided to use. What might work on a street hoodlum would not be the ticket for Pahata, who had a small army of lawyers at her service.

The traffic was heavy, for the faithful had been arriving steadily now throughout the day for the Second Astral Ascendancy, which was due to take place on the weekend. Annie Fuentes had a siren on her pickup and a flashing light. It came with the job. Town council had just voted money for a new wiring job on the light last fall. Agnes Bessie, who was seated next to Annie, was urging her to use it to cut through the traffic on the road leading up to the gates of Rancho Radiance. But Annie was reluctant. It didn't go with her approach.

"I don't know, Agnes. We come in here with our lights flashing and sirens screaming, it's not going to set right."

Agnes looked at her grimly. "Annie, a child is missing! It's a siren situation."

Annie bit her lip. Agnes was right. She turned on her flasher and started the siren and pulled out of the line of traffic. Archie and Coy, who were behind her in their trucks, followed. The three trucks cruised down the highway in the wrong lane. Cars began to pull aside and look at them in wonder. They had not expected this on the advent of the Second Astral Ascendancy. They had heard about the lavender helicopters and the two big jets that Pahata traveled in, but three old rust-bucket pickups, one with a flashing siren, didn't fit into their image of the blissful haven known as Rancho Radiance.

"Are you here to request an audience?" the man said.

"I am the sheriff," Annie Fuentes said firmly. "I am here to question Miss Pahata."

The man visibly winced as he heard her refer to "Miss Pahata."

"Well, usually such arrangements are made through her appointments secretary. Let me go get her."

"You don't seem to understand. I am here as a law enforcement officer. I have a warrant to bring Ms. Pahata in for questioning.

She has the right to have her lawyers present." Oh, for Christ sake, Annie was thinking, I am Mirandizing this dolt. "Would you kindly get Miss Pahata."

The man didn't really know what to do except go directly to Pahata, something he had never in his life done before, but Swami Ben-ji and David Many Hearts were not around. The idea was overwhelming to him. He at least had to find the appointments secretary or a Guardian of the Petal Way. He was really nothing more than a gatekeeper in the main building. "Just a minute," he said.

The appointments secretary was in the Moon Lodge, where men were not welcome, but he knocked on the door, an unheard-of affront. Still, what was the choice but to knock on Pahata's door?

Fifteen minutes later, the posse was ushered into Pahata's presence. It was not the audience chamber or the inner sanctum. It was her upstairs office. She was flanked by two lawyers. Annie had not expected this. She had expected the rock throne, the ladies laying out the flower carpet—all the stuff she had heard about. But not this figure sitting behind a glass and stainless steel desk with lawyers in business suits on either side of her.

"What can we do for you?" One of the lawyers came forward. He had thinning hair and a slight paunch, but he was still young. Not more than forty, tops.

"I'm Annie Fuentes, sheriff of Red Forks and we have some questions that we would like to ask Miss Pahata."

"Yes, go ahead," the other lawyer said quickly.

"Annie," Archie intervened, "aren't you forgetting something?"

"Oh yes . . ." She turned to Miss Pahata. "Miss Pahata, you have the right to remain silent, and anything that you say may be . . ." She stopped dead. Pahata Ra had been looking down at a piece of paper. When she looked up she looked straight at Annie. The iridescent, pupil-less eyes gleamed, empty yet full of terror. Oh my God! Annie thought. Her heart almost stopped.

When she had been an emergency room nurse down in Winslow she thought she had seen everything—bodies mashed up in car wrecks, little kids fried by kerosene stoves, but this was the worst—those eyes. Agnes had to poke her to keep her saying the piece. She finally finished and by that time she had regained some of her composure. She began asking questions.

"I am afraid I just don't know. I've never seen the child."

"But you do say that you know the child's mother." Calista watched grimly. Harriet didn't even turn toward her as she spoke.

"Yes, I knew her slightly at a different time in my life."

"Slightly? We were roommates, Harriet."

"Briefly." Harriet smiled.

"But did you not have a recent interview with Mrs. Jacobs?"

"Yes, she came with a special request for her boyfriend." The two lawyers smirked on cue.

The jerk! Calista thought.

"And Tonk Cullen?" Annie continued.

"I never met Mr. Cullen."

"I believe Mr. Swami did. Might we talk to him now?"

"He is not here."

"And where were you the day before yesterday between, say, the hours of noon and midnight?"

"I . . . I was in Utah. There is a project we have begun working on up there. As a matter of fact, my picture was in the Utah newspapers. Bakkirh, can you get those papers for us." She nodded at the appointments secretary.

Rather quick with her alibi, Archie and Calista both thought at the same time.

"It seems, Miss Pahata," Annie persisted, ignoring the alibi altogether, "that Charley's tracks were found going up to a certain point on a trail off the Old Palatki Wash Road. At a point where they stopped there were signs that a helicopter had landed." Annie paused and waited for a response. "Yes . . . do you have anything to say?"

"No," Pahata answered simply.

"But there were helicopter landing marks there, and you are the only person around here who owns a helicopter."

One of the lawyer stepped forward at this point. "We are not following this line of questioning, Sheriff. Could you be more precise?"

Archie now answered, "I don't see how she can be much more precise."

"We do represent Pahata Ra, Dr. Baldwin. May I advise you that this is not a court of law and that my client does not have to answer any questions at this time."

"Don't worry, John," said Pahata to her lawyer. "I can handle this. Let me try and clarify the question." Then, turning to Archie and smiling, she said, "I don't know what you are suggesting. You say there are tracks, supposedly of the child."

"Not supposedly. They are his."

"I don't see how you can really tell, but even if you could, how does this relate to my helicopter? My chopper goes all over. This is a vast ranch. We're always checking on things. It lights down many places where I am sure there are tracks of many things."

"We're not talking about many tracks. We're talking about one specific set and they were not found on your ranch."

The lawyers exchanged glances and smirked again. Now it was the other one's turn. Mr. Casual. He hunched up his shoulders for the first part of a dismissive shrug, opened his hands palm up in a gesture to indicate the futility of their arguments, and then, with a chuckle that continued under his speech like a current of disdain, of disbelief, said, "Really, Dr. Baldwin, with all due respect, I just don't think you have too much to go on here."

"Well, maybe the district attorney will find more," Archie said grimly.

"The district attorney?" Both lawyers' jaws dropped, and Pahata barely concealed a gasp.

No one really saw that gasp except Calista. And Harriet saw her take notice of it. Calista winked. Harriet glared.

"Gods look funny gasping!" Calista said in a very low voice.
"What's that?" One of the lawyers turned to Calista.
"Nothing."

"I want to talk to her, Archie. I have to!"
"Calista, they aren't going to let you. Did you see how those lawyers whisked her away?"
"It's going to be worse when the district attorney comes," Calista said.
"You're right. But screwing Harriet to the wall is not going to work. She's not going to confess anything. She'll lie through her teeth. We've got to be smarter than she is."
"How are we going to keep hunting for Charley and watch her every movement but not let her know it?"
"She's not going to do anything to arouse suspicion, and you heard Annie say she had to stay put." Annie was standing beside them and nodded.
"If she's desperate, she's going to make some sort of move. We'll watch. We'll wait."
"I'm desperate. I can't wait." Tears began rolling down Calista's face.
Archie put his arm around her. "Don't worry." He put his mouth right up to her ear. "Annie and I have a plan," he whispered.

**47**————————Lucille Greyeyes had lingered in the back of the room during the interrogation routine. She had briefly excused herself to go to the rest room and was not seen again while the posse was still there. When she emerged almost an hour after the posse had left she was wearing a standard-issue Rancho Radiance design—a rainbow-patterned tent fly. It was the same pattern that they used for much of the upholstery

and curtains in their new retreat hotels and spas. Lucille had had
no trouble getting hold of the fabric. She was postmistress of Red
Forks, had been for twenty-five years. Most of her work these
days consisted of dealing with the huge influx of stuff that came
for Rancho Radiance. It was too much work for a one-woman
post office and on the next town council meeting's agenda was
a proposal to have Rancho Radiance send down some people to
help her, seeing as they were the ones who generated most of
this mail. In the meantime Lucille just helped herself to a tent
fly. A whole mess of them had come in for this weekend.

In the restroom, she had taken down her bun and braided her
hair like an old squaw, then put on some little dark glasses. Under
the folds of the tent fly, which she had tied as a kind of toga over
one shoulder, she carried a walkie-talkie. Coy had another one.
He was going to stake out the front entrance. Agnes and Annie
were working as a team covering a back entrance. Archie had
supplied them all with walkie-talkies, ones that he always carried
for his crews to use in the field in case of emergency. Lucille
was to report any movements not only of Pahata but of the two
choppers. One was gone now. If the other were to leave, she was
supposed to report it or any vehicle bearing Pahata. She was also
to keep her eyes peeled for Swami Ben-ji and David Many Hearts.

# 48

The helicopter had been
flying around all that morning. So it had been impossible for
Charley and Tonk to move, in such danger of being spotted.
They had lost some of their good walking time. But worst of all,
Tonk was totally out of it. He did not at this point know who he
was anymore, and Charley felt more lost than ever. Tonk stared
right through Charley, as if he could have been a tree or a rock
or a cloud. He seemed barely aware of Charley as a person. Tonk
might die. Charley had to get himself used to this idea and there

was nothing he could do to stop it. It scared him. He tried to hold Tonk's hand and talk to him softly and remind him of things—but Tonk had lived for ninety years and Charley had only known him for two days, so what was there for him to recall for Tonk? All he could really hope to recall for him was his anger over Claudie and the Pahatties. But Tonk would just stare and occasionally blink as if he were not comprehending a word Charley had said. He couldn't believe that Tonk would let Claudie slip away so completely, because the last coherent conversation he had had with him had been about Claudie. It was not all that coherent, but it was something about her being so pretty and soft like a desert rose. And then he just stopped talking about her. If Charley asked him anything, it was as if he had never even heard the name Claudie.

But despite all this, his instincts for certain things were still keen. Several times he had guided Charley around rattlesnakes, spying them long before Charley did. He seemed to have a kind of generalized sense of imminent danger and he would constantly scan the sky for the chopper.

There was no sign of the helicopter now and the sky had clouded up as if it were about to rain. Charley had certainly never expected any rain out here. He supposed it had to sometime. Maybe they should pack up, try and make up some time. He touched Tonk lightly on the elbow. "Come on, Tonk. Let's get going while the going's good."

Tonk was incredible in this respect. For a man his age he could move well. He was surefooted, and while he had been lucid Charley had learned enough from him about which plants were edible and likely sources for water. They had not even had to touch the water in the canteens. Charley had just paused on a slight rise of land after winding out of a small canyon.

"Watch it there!" They were the first word Tonk had spoken all day. He pointed ahead. There was a rattlesnake just below the path under a clump of mesquite. Charley gingerly walked higher up on the far edge of the path as he passed by. Tonk seemed in a strange way to sense Charley's extreme fear of rattlesnakes, although he had never told him the story of his father's death. It was not something he could readily speak about. He felt he really didn't need to with Tonk anyway.

They had been following a narrow path of sorts against a sheer wall that had been part of the wall of the canyon. But the floor of the canyon had gradually climbed to higher land. On the other side of the path the land, which until now had fallen away quite abruptly, began to slope off at a gentler angle. It almost looked like a prairie, and Charley could see a few grassy expanses that could have supported some grazing animals. Then Charley blinked. He couldn't believe it. There was a fence below him, not thirty feet away. Civilization! There must be a rancher or someone nearby. He scrambled down the incline. A small cascade of rock fragments trailed him. He walked along the fence for twenty, thirty, maybe forty feet, looking for some sign, a property marker, a no-trespassing sign, anything. When he found it the sign was quite small, but unmistakable: two interlocking rainbows. They were at Rancho Radiance. He looked across in disbelief the narrow stretch of land between the ridge behind him and one perhaps a thousand feet away. Melting out of the other rock face were the remnants of walls built on ledges. Cliff dwellings. Wow! It slowly dawned on Charley. He was staring Los Gatos right in the face. Of course! Archie had shown him the map. Los Gatos was on the northwest corner of the Rancho Radiance. At that moment he heard the unmistakable thrumping and the whole sky began to pulsate. The helicopter was back and there was no cover here.

# 49

"I could have sworn that I spotted the kid right here," David Many Hearts was saying.

"They couldn't just have vanished." Swami squinted through his thick lenses.

But they had. Charley was amazed himself. He had not even been aware of Tonk trailing after him when he had come down to look at the fence, but as soon as the chopper appeared he had felt himself being yanked. An iron claw on his shoulder had dragged him into a space that Charley would have never believed they could have fitted into. Tonk was prone on top of him. It was a kind of natural culvert under the path that edged along the wall. There were only twenty inches between the floor of the culvert and the ceiling. But there they were like some sort of human sandwich and above them Fat Ass and Dickhead were walking and wondering where in the hell they could have disappeared to. They had paced this section of the path maybe five times. Little bits of dirt sifted down onto their faces each time they passed over. Charley was still in a somewhat stunned state. He simply could not believe Tonk's reflexes. Here he'd thought the old guy was totally gone, on the brink of death, and he scoped out this place, grabbed Charley, and shoved them both in. Man, all his neurons were firing when you really needed them.

As Charley's stunned disbelief began to ebb it was replaced not by fear but by anger. He had to get these guys. Enough of this defensive stuff. These guys would be back time and time again. He was sick of it. He had to think in terms of offensive strategy. These guys had a chopper, and all Charley could tell so far was that they had one weapon. David Many Hearts was carrying that. Was there any chance of disarming them? Or maybe sabotaging the helicopter? Crash and burn. What a delightful thought.

"Look, their tracks are all over here," David Many Hearts was saying. They had moved farther away down the path.

"I know they must be up this way somewhere."

"Good God! Those fellers couldn't track a herd of elephants through wet sand," Tonk whispered in a low, dusty voice when they were out of earshot. He cackled softly.

"Tonk, you okay? I thought you were a goner."

"Naw, I can sniff danger mile away. These guys are dangerous but they're dumb."

Charley felt something inexpressibly happy ignite inside him. "My thoughts exactly, Tonk! We have to figure out how to fix these bastards but good. I'm sick of running away from them."

"Me too! And I told you what they did with them straws they got buyin' land and how they been pressing Claudie."

Oh, thank God, Charley thought jubilantly. He's back! And for however briefly, he prayed that they would think of something, some way to get these bastards. The idea would have to be to disarm them somehow, render them powerless, though Charley had not altogether rejected the notion of killing them. The first step had to be to get rid of their weapons. And in this sense the helicopter was a weapon. Suddenly Charley had a grisly idea. He felt his own heart quicken and his mouth went dry. He felt his anger too, old anger, well up within him. By God, in the name of his father he would do it.

"Tonk?"

"Yeah, boy."

"Remember that rattlesnake we passed just a little ways back? Right before I went down to look at the fence."

"Yeah."

"Do you think it's still back there?"

"Probably. They don't move round much this time of day."

"Would you know how to pick one up without getting hurt?"

"Oh sure. Nothing to it. You know, horses git bit by them all the time. No harm comes to them, but you got to know how to git 'em loose from the snakes. And I used to catch them for museum and zoo people."

"Okay. I figure that snake's not more than fifty feet away from this spot. I got my backpack here."

"I know. I feel it right in my gut."

"Well, if we move fast, before they come back . . ."

Fat Ass and Dickhead were not only out of earshot now, but they had wound down the steep incline and were becoming very small figures in the canyon. They think we're down there, Charley thought excitedly, because that's where all the good hiding places would be, naturally! Except if you're with Tonk, who Charley was quickly coming to realize was one of the major brains of this century in spite of the fact that occasionally he lost the thread of the conversation. He never, however, lost the thread of life!

# 50 _____ "Okay, it's Lucille, Aggie."

"You've got something?"

"Yeah, she's driving a jeep out the back here. She's not heading for any gate I can see. There seems to be a service road she's following. She's heading north by northwest."

"Oh, that must be the old Mormon road, the one they used when they passed us by."

"It sure looks that way."

"Of course, dear, it cuts right across that property straight up to Los Gatos."

Lucille was not one to argue with Agnes Bessie. As the town historian she knew it all—every trail that indicated the peregrinations of those Mormons, Indians, gold prospectors, or others who had passed through, by, and over Red Forks for whatever reason.

"Okay, well, you tell Archie and I'll keep you informed."

"Any sign of the chopper?"

Agnes was really becoming something—choppers! My goodness. "No, dear."

"Well, I'll tell Archie, roger and out."

"Yes, dear. I mean yes, roger and out."

**51**————————It had all gone well so far, but
Charley had nearly fainted in the process. Tonk had forked up
that snake as if he were flipping pancakes and dumped it into
the bag. They had then carried the bag to the chopper. He had
watched Tonk milk it by using their last orange. He had stared,
fascinated, unable to tear his eyes away from his father's killer.
For years he had tried to drive images like this away. They were
part of his worst nightmares and now he was staring at this head
of death. And the ninety-year-old man was milking it.

"Just take a little of the piss out of it to make it a tad sluggish,
so it'll stay put for while we need it."

They had found a long branch and put it near, but not too
near, the chopper. The branch would provide an instrument for
removing the snake. This was an important part of the plan. They
were counting on David Many Hearts to put down the gun or
prop it when he went to reach for the branch. Swami never
seemed to touch the gun except for when they had dropped the
net over them and he had stood guard while David had fixed the
net.

The plan now was that when the gun was put down Charley
would dash out and get it. He and Tonk were hiding in the ruins
of Los Gatos, the crumbling cliff dwelling. They were near the
edge of the first terrace, crouched behind a low wall. A canti-
levered ceiling of red sandstone cast them in a deep shadow at
this time of the day. The wall was curved and must have at one
time been a part of the kiva, or ceremonial chamber.

Suddenly they saw the two figures emerging on the other side,
back from their search. Their voices carried clearly across to the
cliff dwelling despite the fact that they were still almost one
thousand feet away.

Charley could feel his own heart beating loudly, echoing, it seemed, throughout the silence of the canyon. But he was not afraid. He was finished being afraid. After all, he had looked down into the face of his father's killer, the face of death, when Tonk had forked up that hissing, writhing snake, and he had felt no hatred, nor anger, just sorrow. The hate that he had nurtured for so long had ebbed out of him. He would never stop missing his father, but he felt a new calm and with it a new resolve and strength. He liked the cool rock silence of this dwelling. Archie had described these ancients as being people highly spiritual but decidedly pragmatic. He felt the shadows of these forgotten spirits gathering around him now, pressing in on him with all their strength. Here the Anasazi waited out the winters when the earth died. He could imagine the snow shrouding this landscape, covering these rocks. And now he was waiting, with them. Was it for murder or was it for a new greening, a new chance for life?

# 52

David Many Hearts was the first to reach the chopper, the first to open the door, and his scream was earsplitting. Charley could only imagine that the snake had reared and was ready to strike.

"There's a goddam rattlesnake in there," David roared.

"Shoot it!" Swami cried in a high, piercing voice.

"You're nuts—wanna blow up the chopper, asshole?"

"Well, get the thing out!"

"Get it out, he says!"

This was great! Tonk and Charley looked at each other and grinned. These guys were definitely losing their cool and with their cool would go what few brains they had.

"Look! Look!" Swami was pointing. "There's a big branch over there.

Tonk poked Charley gently in the ribs. They were going for the bait!

"Okay, okay! Keep watch on the chopper. If that thing starts to slither out, tell me." Swami nodded nervously. "Should I hold the gun?"

"No!" David said emphatically. "You'll wind up shooting yourself before the snake or, worse, blow up the goddam chopper."

Perfect!

David Many Hearts started walking toward the branch. It was really a limb from one of the sycamore saplings that was sprouting near the first terrace of the cliff dwelling. To carry it he would have to put down the gun. Charley had made sure that the branch was closer to where he and Tonk were than to the chopper. That way he would wait until David had reached the chopper before running out to pick up the gun.

Okay, put it there, Charley coached silently, atta boy, Dickhead. Now pick up the branch and walk back to the chopper, David Many Farts.

Charley was so intent on watching David Many Hearts that he had not heard the distant noise of a jeep coming up the valley. He did not even see the jeep as it rounded a stand of trees. Tonk nudged him sharply in the ribs. *Holy shit.* He started to scramble over the wall toward the gun, but there wasn't time.

# 53

They stood there frozen, like pieces on a chessboard. David Many Hearts had turned around and spotted Charley coming down for the gun at the same time Pahata drove up.

"Don't move!" she said to Charley. "David, get the gun."

David Many Hearts could not get that gun. That was all Char-

ley could think. He cannot reach that gun. But he was closer to
it than Charley, and Fat Ass was following directly behind him.
Nobody at this moment was armed. Wrong! He, Charley, was
armed! Charley suddenly remembered the sling in his pocket
with two round stones. He slid his hand into the jeans pocket.
The movement was very quick, very smooth, and then his arm
was spinning. Pahata Ra, David, and Swami looked at him transfixed, as if he'd gone crazy. It was a motion totally out of context
for the situation. It looked as if he were winding up to turn a
cartwheel or pitch a baseball.

"Stop!" cried Pahata. But it was too late. David had fallen
clutching his throat. A second stone seemed to explode from
nowhere and shatter Swami's glasses. Then Pahata and Charley
both dived for the shotgun at the same time.

He had to get the gun away from both of them. He had to try
and kick it out of the way before it went off and shot him. She
was squishy and soft under those robes and they were getting all
tangled up. God, he could feel the stock under his back. He'd
get shot, he knew it. Then he heard the explosion! Did he feel
it? They both stopped moving. Was he wounded? Charley
thought of all those movies where guys were shot and didn't even
know it until they saw the pool of blood. There was a second
shot right over their heads.

"Git up!" a voice roared. It was Tonk. He was standing there
with the shotgun and firing into the air.

Charley sprang up and stood by Tonk. Pahata was a crumpled
mass of white silk. She raised her iridescent eyes, baleful and
undaunted, to them.

Charley had spun around to make sure David Many Hearts
and Swami were still disabled. Swami was unconscious, maybe
dead. He'd take a closer look later. David was having trouble
breathing.

"You come for Claudie, didn't ya?"

"What?" Charley wheeled around.

"She's up there," Tonk said in a steady voice. "I found part of her hair ribbon. She tied back her hair with a scrap of blue calico, matched her eyes. Then I saw some bone. Flesh doesn't last long out here specially when you bury 'em shallow like you did in that back kiva."

"Oh my God! Archie! It's him!" Calista cried. She was leaning out of the passenger window of the truck. Three other trucks were right behind them, and overhead there was the staccato sound of a police helicopter. It was just at that moment that Tonk looked up and felt his old fear returning. He forgot the woman at his feet and what it was all about. It was in that instant that Pahata, her robes streaming out behind her, ran. From Calista's point of view, it looked like some crazy bird trying to take flight. She was running straight for the ruins. It happened so quick Charley wasn't ready for it. His hand plunged into his pocket but there were no more stones. Then his mom was there hugging him, and Archie was practically picking them both up. The next thing he knew there were all these state troopers. They seemed to have materialized out of nowhere. They had David Many Hearts and Swami in handcuffs.

"Where'd she go?" one asked.

"Up there." Charley pointed. "She's in the ruins. And, by the way, there's a rattlesnake in the chopper. So be careful."

"Is she armed?" another trooper asked.

"No, I don't think so. She sure wanted this gun."

The other troopers had begun to go into the ruin.

"I have to go," Calista said.

"No, Cal." Archie put a hand on her shoulder.

"No, I have to. I have to see her face now when they catch her."

Charley knew exactly what his mother meant. It was the same as his need to look at the snake when Tonk had forked it up. Archie should let her go, he thought, because then she'll stop hating. You can't keep on hating. It takes too much energy.

Calista had pulled herself loose from Archie's grip and ran to catch up with the troopers.

Harriet had wedged herself into a high, narrow place on the third level. It was a precarious place. They couldn't reach her and she was not in good range for the sharpshooters either. A sergeant came down.

"She wants to see Mrs. Jacobs. Says she'll come out if she can first talk to you." He nodded toward Calista.

"Don't!" Archie barked. "I don't want you going up there."

"We can keep her covered, Dr. Baldwin."

"I don't like it."

"Archie, I'm going. I've got to look this monster in the face."

"She'll come down eventually."

"We've all got better things to do," Calista said emphatically.

The chief, a large, burly fellow, took off his hat and wiped his brow with his sleeve. "Why don't we wait a little while and see. He's right, ma'am. She might come out sooner than you think."

But she didn't It was getting near sunset, the time of the day when the Hopis let the last rays wash away the cares and weariness of the day. Calista looked at Archie. "I'm going up."

Archie had never in his life been so scared. He watched the slender figure of the person he loved most disappear into the ruins. The fact that there were three sharpshooters posed on the walls covering her did nothing to relieve his fears. Who knew what that crazy woman would do?

"So you came?" The voice frightened her. She could see nothing of Harriet. It emanated from a shadowy crack high up in a wall. How had she ever gotten up there, let alone wedged herself in? Calista felt her mouth grow dry. She swallowed.

"Yes, I came. Now what's this all about?" She said this in her sharpest no-nonsense voice.

"Step closer." Calista hesitated. It had to be a trap. But she wanted to see her. She had this inexorable need to see the face of this horrible creature who had kidnapped her son. "They've got me covered, Harriet. So don't try anything. Half the state militia is here. They have sharpshooters."

"Yeah, I know," Harriet said with a laugh. Well, Calista certainly did give her points for keeping cool.

"Just step up here a few yards so we can see each other to talk."

It didn't seem like such a high risk. She took four or five steps forward. Just then one of the sharpshooters said, "Not so far, Mrs. Jacobs." Shit! She must be out of their line of fire or something. That was Calista's last coherent thought.

Suddenly it seemed a chunk of the earth collapsed on her. She fell to the ground. There was a ton of dirt and something on top of her. How come nobody was coming to help her? There were no shots, nothing. Something was on top of her shoving her face into the dirt. She felt something tearing . Oh, her eyes! Her eyes felt terrible. God, she was nothing without her eyes! I can't see! I can't see!" she was screaming.

"We're going to die together!" Harriet's voice rasped in her ear.

Then something exploded in her. She opened her jaws as wide as she could and bit. There was a terrible scream. The weight rolled off her. She stood up. They were on an extension of the terrace, a ledge that hung precariously over the deep well of an enormous kiva. Calista's eyes were streaming but she could see Harriet now. She was scrambling up the wall behind her. There were plenty of handholds. She heard the fire of one of the sharpshooters. Not so sharp, she thought slowly as she saw Harriet continue to scramble. Shit! This woman was not going to get away. Calista lunged for her on the wall. She grabbed one ankle. Harriet was kicking furiously. Calista hung on. But then she felt a kick right in her temple and fell backward. Up again. She started clawing the wall after her. She reached the top just as Harriet turned around. Harriet rushed toward her to shove her back down, but in one quick lateral sweep of her arm chopped her right across the ankles. Harriet pitched forward head first over the wall and lay in a crumpled heap on the ledge below.

. . .

The sharpshooters were there and so were Archie and Charley.

Harriet rolled over to see the three gun barrels inches from her face, which was bleeding profusely. But she didn't seem to notice them. Her eyes sought out Calista. She had lost one of her contact lenses in the fray. So now one iridescent eye and one rather mud-colored brown eye looked up. "Luck, Cal. You always had all the luck, didn't you?"

Calista stared hard into the face. She found it fascinating in its emptiness, its lack of any kind of affect. It was totally devoid of any emotional content. The most impressive aspect of the face was its utter and monumental indifference—indifference to life, indifference to feeling. The more she stared at it the more the face began to cease to have any human dimensions. She could be staring at a rock, an inanimate object or some sort of very ancient but little evolved life form—a dull-witted predator, venomous, with a small brain only designed for killing—conscienceless killing.

As Archie led her back down through the ruin she heard Annie Fuentes Mirandizing Pahata. "You have the right to remain silent. . . the right to a lawyer. Anything you say may be held against you in a court of law. . . ."

Annie's soft voice was soon just a scratch in the night that seemed to have engulfed the beautiful valley. Calista looked around at the lovely masonry of the walls of Los Gatos. She walked by Tonk and gave him a pat on the shoulder. Charley stopped and sat down on the wall next to him and held his hand. A police detective was marking off the area where Claudia Perkins's body had been buried. Tonk was lost in a soft reverie of blue hair ribbons and a face like a desert rose, but he could not remember where it was or why these people were calling him Tonk or why he felt this funny, sad unplaceable feeling. But he had touched her skin and he had known the desert rose and that was all a man needed to know or feel after almost a century on this earth. That was living.

**54**———————————Agnes Bessie had tacked down
the black velvet on the chip board and had just finished polishing
the case with some Windex. Now came the fun part, putting in
the arrowheads. She had an arrangement all in mind. First she'd
start with the Clovis points and then put in a row of her four
best Pinto points. She had some real nice Folsom ones too. She
guessed she should really go in chronological order left to right
beginning with the Clovis and then to the Folsom. She picked
up a point and put it on the black velvet. My, didn't it look
pretty. Archie had gotten this case sent up from Phoenix even
though the museum wouldn't be ready to open for another year
or so. She was going to start getting exhibits ready. The town
council had voted the funds and Archie himself had kicked in
five thousand dollars. That took care of the roof repairs right
there. The contractors were going to start next week. In the
meantime she had to beef up the settler part of the exhibit. She
was loaded with Indian stuff, but seeing as so few had settled
here there wasn't much in the way of those kinds of artifacts.
She had some old Victorian button shoes in a trunk upstairs that
had belonged to Bert's mother. And there were some old fans,
as well as a leghorn bonnet that she was reconstructing. She had
to call Sissy over in Jerome and see if she had anything more
from Grandma Bessie's attic. She'd like to get her hands on some
old foundation garments—a real nice corset with steel busks and
elastic gussets. There was a knock at the door. Agnes slid the last
arrowhead in. "Come on in. It's open."

Coy McSparrow walked through. "Got something for you,
Aggie."

"What's that, dear?"

"Invitation to a hangin'."

"Whose, Pahata Ra's?"

"Naw, this one here's for the museum."

"What hanging? There was never a hanging here. Least, not that I know about."

"Over in Golden. But that can count, can't it? Same county and all."

"Sure. Let me see it." Coy took out a yellowed piece of paper.

Agnes fished her specs out of the front of her dress where they dangled from a ribbon. Coy tried not to peek, but she had a nice bosom, Agnes. Specially for such a scrawny thing. She put on her specs and began reading.

"Golden, Arizona, November 3, 1899

"You are hereby cordially invited to attend the hanging of Lester Bingham, Murderer. His soul will swing into eternity on November 10, 1899 at 2 o'clock, P.M. sharp.

"Latest improved methods in the art of scientific strangulation will be employed and everything possible will be done to make the proceedings cheerful and the execution a success.

Signed,

F. M. Lebow, Mayor

"F. M. Lebow. He was a cousin of Bert's. Never cared for him much."

"Yeah, well, I thought you might like it anyway for the museum."

"Oh sure."

"Hey, lookee that!" Agnes said, craning her head around Coy and peering out the front door. Two young people on ladders were painting out the Psychic Pilgrim Inn sign from the hotel. Coy turned around.

"Oh yeah. Annie's nephews came over to help do that."

"Well, thank heavens!"

They both stood in the doorway of Agnes's house and watched the boys paint out the sign letter by letter. Behind the hotel, the east wall of the canyon turned a raging red as the sun set beyond the Palatki cliffs. They felt washed and cleansed, ready for a new day.

# 55

————————————————"I can't believe Charley's already on the phone with Amy. He just got back two hours ago from California."

"Well, it was a six-hour trip," said Archie, who was sitting in the wing chair in Calista's study. "So that is eight hours without talking. That's a long time."

"I told him he should invite her for Thanksgiving," Calista said. She had two pencils stuck in her hair and was now working with pen and ink. This was a favorite drawing of hers. She had been looking forward to doing it. It was the one with Wendy coming out of the house Peter had built for her after she had been accidentally shot by one of the lost boys. But there was something too tight about the drawing. She had worked too hard on the pencil sketch and now nothing was flowing. The branches that made the structure had to be gnarlier, the foliage looser but thicker. The house had to look as if it were actually more growing than constructed. She suddenly thought of those Hopi villages Archie had told her about that grew from the earth like the old trees and the houses with deep tap roots fed by labor and ritual. She looked up at Archie, who was watching her.

His wonderful blue eyes looked even bluer because of his tan. A slash of sunlight fell across his jaw from the west facing window in the alcove of the study. She looked at him and smiled. She stuck her pen back in the ink bottle, got up, and walked over to him. He pulled her down onto his lap. She forgot about Peter and Wendy and Never-Land and the gaudy splendor of that other land. She thought only of the top roots of this house on James Place in Cambridge, Massachusetts, and that they were all here together now, nightmares vanquished, hatreds dissolved. Here together. The blade of sunlight fell across both of their faces.

ABOUT THE AUTHOR

Kathryn Lasky Knight is the author of many children's books as well as the Calista Jacobs mysteries *Trace Elements* and *Mortal Words*. She lives with her husband, Christopher Knight, and their two children in Cambridge, Massachusetts, where she is at work on her next Calista Jacobs mystery.